# "What are you really doing here, Beth?" Garrett asked.

The words rumbled between them, quiet yet urgent. "Why come back here, where you hate it so much you could hardly wait to run away?"

"I never hated it here! I just couldn't stay." Beth swallowed down the rest of the words, knowing it wouldn't do any good. He was determined to see her as the enemy.

Fine. She could take that. What she couldn't take was delving back into it all over again, trying to figure out if she'd been wrong to take the opportunity Denis had offered and run with it, to listen to Mr. Winthrop's advice and get out of Gar's life before she ruined it. She hadn't made a mistake; she'd done the right thing. The elegant businessman standing in front of her was proof positive of that.

*You can never go back.* She reminded herself of Denis's oft-used phrase. *But God will lead you on.*

**Books by Lois Richer**

Love Inspired

*A Will and a Wedding* #8
†*Faithfully Yours* #15
†*A Hopeful Heart* #23
†*Sweet Charity* #32
*A Home, a Heart, a Husband* #50
*This Child of Mine* #59
\*Baby on the Way #73
\*Daddy on the Way #79
\*Wedding on the Way #85

†Faith, Hope & Charity
*Brides of the Seasons

## LOIS RICHER

lives in a small Canadian prairie town with her husband who, she says, is a "wanna-be farmer." She began writing in self-defense, as a way to escape. She says, "Come spring, tomato plants take over my flower beds, no matter how many I 'accidentally' pull up or 'prune.' By summer I'm fielding phone calls from neighbors who don't need tomatoes this fall. Come September, no one visits us and anyone who gallantly offers to take a box invariably ends up with six. I have more recipes with tomatoes than with chocolate. Thank goodness for writing! Imaginary people with imaginary gardens are much easier to deal with!"

Lois is pleased to present this latest book in her series BRIDES OF THE SEASONS for the Steeple Hill Love Inspired line. Please feel free to contact Lois at: Box 639, Nipawin, Saskatchewan, Canada S0E 1E0.

# Wedding on the Way
## Lois Richer

♥ *Love Inspired*®

Published by Steeple Hill Books™

STEEPLE HILL BOOKS

Steeple
Hill™

ISBN 0-373-87085-X

WEDDING ON THE WAY

Copyright © 1999 by Lois Richer

**Printed in U.S.A.**

Be strong and take heart,
all you who hope in the Lord.
—*Psalms* 31:24

# *Chapter One*

One year and three months after Beth Ainslow's return to Oakburn, betrayal still burned in Garrett Winthrop's craw. Though he'd done everything he could to ignore her, the petite strawberry-blonde just wouldn't leave his mind alone. Especially since they'd once been engaged, but she'd left him to marry someone else.

Gar had continued to date Cynthia Reardon for a while, but soon realized how foolish that had been. He couldn't go out with one woman when his mind was busy with thoughts of another.

He leaned back in the booth of the local café and heaved a sigh of disgust. How had the presence of one delicate five-foot bit of femininity managed to wreak such havoc on his always calm, always well-organized life?

"I can't believe you didn't tell me she was moving back to town." Gar stirred his coffee three extra times before finally laying down the spoon and facing his friend. "You owed me that, Clay."

Clayton Matthews pushed back his cap and surveyed his friend with a cheeky grin. "Believe me, if I'd known her return would get you this upset, I would have alerted you. But it's been over a year now—you should be used to her. Besides, I've been a little busy with my own love life, remember?" Clay grinned the happily smug smile of a man newly married.

That blissful glow irritated Gar immeasurably. He gulped a mouthful of the steaming brew and winced as it stung all the way down.

"Anyway, what's the problem?" Clay pretended to hide his mocking smile behind his mug. "Are you still carrying a torch?"

"No!" Gar slammed his cup onto the table, and then flushed as every eye in the place focused on him. "It's just that she waltzes back into town, and first thing you know, she's got her finger in every pie. Take that downtown restoration idea we've been working on."

"*You* take it. I'm a farmer, I don't know diddly about downtown restorations."

And Clay seemed totally opposed to learning more, Garrett decided privately.

He forged ahead anyway, intent on proving his point. "What right did she have to advise the Forsyths to sell their building instead of rent it? I've been working with them for months, I know their situation, and even I didn't say that."

"Maybe you should have. She has the right of a

woman with a perfectly good brain, Gar. And she's not afraid to use it. Maddie and Harold Forsyth are in their sixties. They want to travel, not get tied down to renters and renovations. Besides, according to coffee row, Beth aims to buy that building someday. The present location of her flower shop is a little small, I hear.''

Garrett jerked upright, his eyebrows rising. ''What? How would she buy it? Did she suddenly inherit a fortune or something?''

Clay shrugged. ''Beats me. All I know is what I hear.''

''Well, good old Denis Hernsley wasn't rich. I checked.'' As soon as he said it, Gar felt like an oaf for talking that way about Beth's deceased husband. He winced as Clay's eyebrows lifted. Money was not a measure of a man's stature. He knew as well as the next guy—and better than most—that a few dollars in your pocket meant nothing when it came to true happiness.

''Sorry, Clay. I just meant that she had to have money come from somewhere to start the flower thing.'' He frowned, trying to puzzle it out.

''Insurance money, I s'pose. And it's a good thing she got it, too.'' Clay shook his head in disgust. ''Jordan Andrews told me that his wife Caitlin, as a friend, asked Beth to move into Wintergreen because she was homeless. She and her sister Ronnie were living in one of those company houses way up north in Alberta. When Denis died in an oil rig accident, the oil company absolved themselves of the necessity to provide housing, and Beth and Ronnie were out in the cold. So to speak.''

''Ronnie? Veronica was living with them all this time?'' Garrett hadn't heard that before. ''I thought she went to an aunt after her dad got sick a few years back. Why would she be living with Beth and not her father? The girl's underage. She's only fifteen!''

Clay scratched his forehead. ''I don't believe Ronnie's lived with Mervyn since Beth left town. And I can understand why. He was an awful old coot when he'd had a drink. Besides, he used to disappear for days. That's no life for a kid.''

Garrett didn't understand any of this. For the past fifteen months his younger brother Ty and Ronnie, who was now fourteen, had spent most of their time together, a good part of it at his parents' home, Fairwinds. So why hadn't he heard about this before?

Gar was sure someone—his dad maybe—had told him all those years ago that Veronica had gone to live with an aunt. Why would Beth have dragged her little sister along when she herself was only eighteen, a new bride, and hardly prepared for caring for someone else? He cast back in his mind as something twigged his memory…

''We'll have to take in Veronica.''

He could still see it so clearly. She'd called the dorm several times before Christmas that year, asking over and over when he'd be home. Involvement in the drama department and a production they were staging took every spare moment Gar could afford. He hadn't wanted to abandon it before the final performance, so he'd put her off, promising to return for a weekend, an afternoon, lunch together, and then changing his mind at the last minute.

How many times had he wished he'd changed his answer that last day? How often did he hear, over and over, the desperation in her, but he'd gone over it too many times. It was over, done with. Why couldn't he just leave it alone?

"Why're you asking me all this stuff? Why don't you ask her yourself? She's coming in now." Clay swallowed the last of his coffee and searched his pockets for his wallet. "I've got to go. Got a little project on the go and I need some hinges. Take it easy, Gar."

"Yeah. Right." Gar watched Clay pay his bill at the old-fashioned register and walk out the door. What he wouldn't give for such a simple life, and time to do the things he loved most. He'd devoted so much time to the bank—and for what? His father's approval? Approval that never seemed to come, no matter how hard he tried.

Gar stuffed down the traitorous thought. How foolish. He was perfectly happy working at his father's bank. It was Beth's fault he was questioning himself—

"Are you leaving?" Beth's tentative voice roused him from his daydream. "I don't mean that you should. It's just that the place is full, and I thought if you were going—" She stopped, took a deep breath and shook her head. "Never mind. I'll wait."

Gar reached out and grabbed her arm, halting her

progress away from him. It was time to forget the past, to move on.

"Have a seat," he offered quietly. "I wanted to talk to you anyway."

"Thanks. I think." She frowned, peering at him from beneath her lashes.

It could have been ten years ago, Gar decided. She looked barely a day older, except that now she wore her hair short, in a sort of pixie cut, instead of that bouncing blond-red ponytail. Her slight compact form still looked great in jeans and a shirt, and she still darted around like a sparrow.

It was only when he looked into her eyes that he saw a change. When she stared back at him, Gar saw something in those blue depths that made him wince. She'd been hurt. Because he'd avoided her?

"How are you?" She accepted the menu and a cup of coffee from the waitress and added a liberal amount of sugar and cream. "I haven't seen you for months. Been busy?"

"Not as busy as you." He couldn't stop the burst of words. "What right did you have to advise my clients to go against my advice?"

She blinked. "Your clients? Your advice?"

Gar clenched his jaw. "You know very well that the Forsyths have been meeting with me for months to discuss their property."

"Oh. Actually, I didn't." She placed her order and then leaned back against the seat. "I simply asked them if they were thinking of selling their building, and they told me they'd rather rent. That's when I found out they were planning on traveling, and I said I didn't think they'd want to be bothered with renters.''

"So you told them to take the money and run, whether it was a good price or not.'' He nodded, his voice pinched tight. "Yes, I'm aware of your sentiments on the matter.''

She laughed, a light tinkling sound that grated on his nerves. Her eyes were wide with innocence.

"I don't have any sentiments, Gar. I just wanted to know about the building.''

"You couldn't afford it even if they did want to sell.'' He immediately regretted saying it, but there was no way to recall the harsh words.

"Really?'' She looked at the sandwich set before her and immediately removed the pickles. "So what are you so cranky about then? Did I step on your toes by asking about it?''

"I'm not 'cranky'.'' He stopped, lowered his voice and searched desperately for some measure of control. "I am not cranky. I am merely asking you not to counter my advice to *my* clients.''

"Okay.'' She nodded once, then took a dainty bite of the sandwich and chewed appreciatively. "This is so good. I never roast a chicken anymore.''

"I didn't know you knew how. You never used to cook much.'' Gar clamped his lips shut. When would he learn to forget the past?

Beth shrugged. "You never used to be so crabby. Things change.'' She took another bite. "Do you go away in January? I remember your folks always used to leave Minnesota to go to Arizona when it got cold. It's certainly been cold enough since Christmas.''

"I'm not in my dotage yet," he muttered dryly. "And I have no desire to play bingo, bridge or whist for hours on end."

"Nobody said you had to go *there*." She grinned. "Though I don't know how you could resist. All those seniors with their money just sitting gaining interest. Don't you salivate over the prospect of investing it for them?"

Gar glared at her. "You used to worry about money a lot more than I did," he reminded her dourly. "You were always fussing about how much things cost."

"That was then." Beth took a sip of her coffee before she studied him with that thoughtful look he remembered so well. "I've realized that money doesn't matter one iota when it comes to happiness. There are far more important things." She shrugged. "'The Lord giveth and the Lord taketh away.'"

Gar shifted uncomfortably, not liking the question he was going to ask, but needing the answer. "How's business at the Enchanted Florist?"

"A little slow since Christmas, but actually, not bad. I projected my sales to be a little lower, just in case, so I'm doing fairly well. Why?"

She blinked those innocent green eyes at him, and Garrett felt like a creep. "Just wondering. The Forsyths seemed to think you were looking to expand."

She nodded. "I am. The place I've rented is far too small. I didn't realize I'd need so much counter space to work." Beth rolled her eyes. "My assistants and I nearly killed each other before Christmas. There were so many arrangements to be done, we had to take shifts.''

She nibbled the last bit of sandwich away from the crust and daintily covered the leftover edges with her napkin, exactly as she would have done ten years ago.

Garrett couldn't help smiling. So much had changed, and yet so little.

''Why are you asking?'' Her eyes drew his attention.

''I just wondered how—I mean, well—'' he felt his cheeks burn, and looked away from her inquisitive expression ''—I was just wondering.''

''You want to know how I can afford it.'' She plunked her mug on the table and glared at him. ''Where did I get the money? That's it, isn't it?''

He nodded finally, feeling like a firsthand louse.

''Well, don't worry about it, Gar. I didn't walk away from my marriage to Denis with a bag full of money, though he was a good provider. In fact, it's a lot more expensive to run the shop than I'd originally planned on. Especially when I have to freight everything in.''

He felt like a heel for questioning her. Vainly Gar tried to backtrack. ''It doesn't matter.''

Beth held up one hand. ''No, you asked, therefore, you want to know. I don't know how I'd afford to buy it. I'm just trusting God day by day. Where He leads, I'll follow.''

Gar could hardly believe he was hearing this from the woman who once couldn't go an hour without planning exactly when she had to be home. This laissez-faire approach bothered him.

"I suppose I'd have to ask for a loan." She got up from the table and dug in her purse. "I'll know better when the time comes. Right now, I have to concern myself with supporting Ronnie until she's finished college."

"I wanted to ask you about that." Gar lurched to his feet, dug in his pocket and tossed a bill on the table, ignoring her frown of protest. "Clay said you had Ronnie with you after you were married. What's with that?"

He held her arm to escort her through the crowd and out the door, but Beth jerked free and whirled to face him, her eyes glittering with some suppressed emotion.

"Does it really matter, Garrett? I left Oakburn, got married, and Ronnie lived with us. Okay? That's in the past. Why don't you just let it go?"

Gar saw Beth's cheeks flush bright red as she became aware of the stares of the other patrons. She strode quickly across the room and out the door, trying to ignore them all.

This time his height and long legs gave him an edge, and Garrett used it to good advantage. He followed her out of the café and caught up with her as she jaywalked across the street.

"I can't let it go because I feel like you're hiding something. I thought it then, too, but I brushed it off. Now I need to know what happened all those years ago." He peered straight into her eyes.

"Please level with me, Beth. I think you owe me that much."

He could see the fire lick into her eyes. He could feel the defensiveness as she straightened to her full five-foot-two-inch height. Most of all, he could hear the anger as she spoke, carefully enunciating every word.

"I owe you?" Her emerald eyes dared him to repeat it. "I owe you nothing, Garrett Winthrop. We were going to be married, but the timing wasn't right. You needed to finish school, and I needed to do other things. God led us down different paths. You and I made our decisions ten years ago."

"But that's just it," he protested, his frustration growing. "I didn't make any decision." He frowned. "I'm just trying to understand, Beth."

"I think it's better if you focus on accepting the past, and move on. I'm going to."

With that she turned and shoved the door to her shop open, pausing for one tiny moment to cast a look over her shoulder. As he searched her eyes, Gar thought he saw something there that looked remarkably like pain. But that couldn't be, could it?

Beth had dumped *him,* not the other way around.


"The nerve of that man!"

Beth flounced around her apartment later that night in a fit of pique, straightening things that didn't require straightening as she vented to her two friends. "I owe him? Hardly!"

"What on earth did the poor man say that triggered this?'' Maryann Matthews asked, cutting through Beth's stormy thoughts.

"It was more what he hinted. As if I owe it to him to explain my life history just because we once dated!''

"Beth, you have to admit you did a little more than date.'' Caitlin offered her admonishment quietly. "You were going to marry the man, remember?''

"Yes, but he didn't want that. He found someone else. I know that for a fact. Never mind how.'' She held up a hand, forestalling the questions written all over their faces. "It was over. And it still is, so don't get any ideas.''

Beth glared at Maryann and Caitlin, daring them to mention any matrimonial plans they might have for her. When they simply blinked at her, she flopped onto her rickety used sofa with a sigh.

"The whole town has informed me that Garrett Winthrop and Cynthia Reardon are the perfect couple. She's the perfect kind of woman for him—so pleasant, so smart, so finished. As if I can't see that for myself.'' Beth glared down at her ragged sweats and made a face. "But sometimes I wonder what I'm even doing here. What does God want from me?''

"I guess we'd all like to know that upfront.'' Maryann sipped her coffee, her face thoughtful. "Unfortunately, that's not usually the way it works.''

"I wanted to have a new beginning here—a fresh start. I wanted Ronnie to have a place that was good to grow up in, a place she could get to know Dad without all the awful history. I wanted to give her good memories." Beth sighed. "Everything seemed so simple when we were up north."

"It always does." Caitlin's eyes were shaded. "Maryann thought it would be easy to come back, I thought it would be easy to put the past behind me. I guess it's a group thing with us." She chuckled. "The Widows of Wintergreen. It's as if the old house is some kind of refuge for wayward widows who need to get over their past hang-ups!"

"In a way, maybe it is." Beth chewed on the edge of the blackened cookie her sister had gleefully presented earlier. "It's the one place we can get reacclimatized to life in this Minnesota town. Get beyond the past."

"I'm not sure it's that easy, Beth." Maryann got up to saunter over to the window. "Before I married Clay, I'd been trying to put the past behind me. The thing is, it just won't stay there. It affects the present and the future, even though we wish it didn't."

Beth shifted uncomfortably. She knew Maryann had suffered in her first marriage, although the other woman had never said much. But life back in high school couldn't have been as hard for Maryann and Caitlin as it had been for her.

"Maybe we've gone about things the wrong way. Maybe we should have just laid it all on the table and tried to go on from there, instead of hiding the hurt. I don't know." Maryann returned to her seat.

"I don't want to talk about the past," Beth insisted. "I want to talk about the future, as I see it."

"And that future doesn't include Gar?" Caitlin's eyebrows lifted.

"How can it? He's not in my league, he's got his own life now. And it includes someone else." Beth faced her friends' curious looks. "Not that that's important. I didn't expect him still to be single. I thought he'd have married one of those debutantes he saw at college. I thought he'd have kids by now."

Maryann made a face. "Garrett was head over heels in love with you, Bethy. He didn't even know the rest of the female population was alive. I don't suppose he could turn that off the day you left. It must have been very difficult for him. Even Cait and I didn't understand why you had to go so quickly." Her blue eyes darkened. "I do know you weren't in love with Denis. Not at first."

"No, I wasn't. I think I stopped believing in that kind of love the day Garrett refused to marry me." She cast her mind back to the first days of her marriage and smiled. "Denis helped me get past that. He was a wonderful man, you know."

"You're avoiding the truth, Beth." Caitlin shook her head vehemently. "You can't just toss out something like love by merely declaring that you won't feel it anymore. Tell us what you really believe, honey. Are you still carrying a torch for Gar?"

They wouldn't give up. She knew that much about her high school friends. They'd keep probing until they got an answer. But how could she admit that after all this time, after being virtually ignored by Garrett for more than a year, she had realized he still held a piece of her heart? How could she deal with that without opening herself up to the same questions she'd asked ten years ago?

Sure, she had her own business now, was self-sufficient, had learned that she was worth caring about. But she still wasn't the kind of person who lived in the Winthrop mansion, wore silk and cashmere, and held afternoon teas and glittering soirees.

"I can never go back, Caitlin. Maybe you and Maryann are different, I don't know. But for me, I've learned what my deficiencies are, and I'm still not the kind of wife that Gar needs." She tossed the burned cookie back onto the plate and picked up her hot chocolate.

She'd have to tell a bit of it, Beth decided. They wouldn't give in until she did.

"I'm from the wrong side of the tracks, girls. My father is a drunk who never got over my mom's death. When he went on a bender, it wasn't a lot of fun."

The two pretty faces across the room were distorted by frowns of disbelief.

"Beth, honey." Caitlin's voice brimmed with compassion. "I always knew there was something wrong, but we never guessed this. I'm so sorry."

"I know. So was I." She refused to cry.

"Me, too." Maryann got up to offer a quick hug. "I suppose we should have asked more questions, probed a little more."

"It wouldn't have mattered." Beth sighed wearily. "I wouldn't have told you anyway. It was my shame to bear."

"Why your shame?" Caitlin was frowning.

"Your father drank, not you. Besides, everybody gets hurt in life. It's part of living in this world."

"Part of living a certain way, maybe. I'll guarantee Gar never had to be embarrassed about his father's actions. The Winthrops are the perfect picture of civic responsibility, the perfect married couple, the perfect parents. They have the same hopes and dreams, they share a common history. No one looks at his father and shakes his head in disgust."

Beth swallowed down the welling of self-pity that rose inside, and carefully set her cup on the table. She choked over her next words, the pain building inside as she pretended fact was fiction. There were some things she just couldn't tell even her best friends. "Imagine, just for a moment, if Dad staggered into one of those fancy dress balls the Winthrops hold every Valentine's! Gar would have been humiliated by me even before Dad opened his mouth and started his ugly diatribe."

The stunned looks on the other women's faces told her how well she'd kept his secret. They thought this was a hypothetical situation. Of course, they would. They'd been long gone from town when that had happened.

"Beth! I didn't realize it was that bad. Did he *hurt* you?" Caitlin's voice was barely audible.

"No. He wasn't that kind of a drunk. He'd rant and rave, then disappear for days. We never knew when he'd come back, or even *if* he'd come back." Her voice dropped in embarrassment. "Sometimes he was gone so long, we'd run out of things. The scariest part was the not knowing." Beth shivered, remembering those long dark nights.

"I couldn't stay and live that way with Ronnie seeing so much ugliness. So one day, before he passed out, I got him to sign her care over to me." She shrugged, pretending the entire matter was of absolutely no consequence. "Then I went looking for a job to support us both."

"Why didn't you tell someone?" Maryann stood and paced the length of the room. "There were people who could have helped."

Beth shook her head, her face tight with the effort of retaining control. "Uh-uh, Mare. I couldn't face the embarrassment. The whole town was already gossiping about the white trash Gar was engaged to. I couldn't make it any worse for them. Besides, his dad…" She stopped, glancing from one to the other. "It doesn't matter anymore now. It's finished." What was the point in delving back into it all over again, trying to figure out if she'd been wrong to take the opportunity Denis had offered when Gar was away at school and run with it, to listen to Mr. Winthrop's advice and get out of Gar's life before she ruined it.

Maryann shifted uncomfortably on her chair, her forehead pleated in a frown. "The youth group could have prayed for you—helped you."

"Do you think I didn't pray?" Beth let the hoarse laugh escape. "I prayed almost hourly for some way of escape. Sometimes I was so afraid to leave Ronnie alone, I took her with me on some of our dates.

Gar didn't seem to mind back then.'' She shrugged. ''But God didn't answer my prayers.''

''How do you know?''

Beth smiled sadly as she shook her head at Caitlin. ''I was there, remember? I lived through it.''

''But, Bethy, maybe that's the answer. Maybe God meant for you to meet and marry Denis. You had a good marriage, didn't you?''

''Yes, in a way. We cared for each other, and he was the kindest, most caring person I could have asked for Ronnie to grow up with. He understood me. I guess that could have been part of God's plan, for Denis to take care of us. Right?'' She fiddled with her hands, ignoring the satisfied looks Maryann and Caitlin exchanged as she tried to reason it out in her mind.

''Did you ever tell Gar about your dad?'' The question came softly, surprising her.

''No!'' She stared at them. ''Of course not. How could I? I didn't want him to know about all that ugliness. Anyway, I'm sure he heard it around town. Everyone knew Mervyn Ainslow tipped the bottle too often.'' Even now the stigma of being the daughter of the town's drunk stung.

''We didn't!'' Maryann's eyes were wide and unblinking. ''But we're veering off the subject. We want to know how you feel about Gar now.''

''I don't know. I still find him attractive. I think he's done very well for himself. I want the best for him.'' Beth gathered up the rumpled napkins and used cups, loading them all on the tray she'd painted about this time last year. "I can't really tell you any more than that."

Tears filled her eyes as she carried the tray into the kitchen and disposed of the dishes in the sink full of soapy water. She could hear the other two moving about, and she searched desperately for a shred of composure.

"Bethy? I think God brought you back here to face the past and find out something about yourself." Caitlin's voice sounded behind her as warm caring arms hugged her close. "I'm sure if you told Gar why you needed to leave, that you had to find work—"

"No! You two are not to say a word of this to anyone. Promise?" She whirled around to glare at them both, urging them with her eyes to support her on this. "I don't want to resurrect the past. I'm trying to maintain my self-esteem in this town and show them that Beth Ainslow isn't worthless. I'm not smart, but I went to college and graduated, even if it was night school and by correspondence. I'm not some poor pitiable creature anymore. Let Garrett think what he likes about me, if he thinks about me at all. I don't care. Neither does he."

"But you do care, sweetie. That's why it still hurts." Maryann sighed when Beth shook her head. "And you're focusing on the wrong things. Self-worth doesn't come from your roots, or what people think about you, or even from the pain you've endured. It comes from knowing your value to God and what you make of what He gives you. Believe me, I know that better than most."

Beth started to protest, but Maryann held up a hand. "All right. If that's the way you want it, I promise I won't say a word. Not that I see Gar much anymore. Life on the farm doesn't allow for many chance encounters."

"You love it and you know you do," Caitlin giggled. "And your new husband just loves showing off his new furniture upstairs. It's a good thing your father-in-law decided to rent the place after you two got married, Maryann."

"Willard likes being on his own. And it's easier for us, too." Maryann's troubled gaze met Caitlin's, and some secret message Beth couldn't interpret passed between the two.

"Promise me, Caitlin. Not one word to Garrett or anyone else about the past. Promise." Beth refused to look away, and sighed with relief when Caitlin finally nodded.

"I think it's a mistake, Beth. But if that's what you want, I won't go against your wishes. I just wish—"

"If wishes were horses, I'd be a rancher." Beth smiled at them both to show that she wasn't suffering. "I'm too old to believe in fairy-tale endings anymore, girls. There's not going to be a prince to sweep me off my feet and carry me to his castle." She frowned. "I don't even want there to be. I just want to get on with the future." She followed them out of the kitchen.

"I know you're hurt." Caitlin handed Maryann her coat and pulled open the apartment door. "But most of the time, the future and the past are interwoven. You're a product of the past, Beth, but with God's help, you can rise above any circumstance and build a future that shows the real you." She leaned down and pressed a kiss against Beth's cheek. "Night, Bethy. Thanks for the cookies. I won't ask for the recipe."

"Funny. Very funny. I'll tell Ronnie you loved them. That way she'll make you guys a batch of your own burned ones for her next home-economics project." Beth grinned at Caitlin's less-than-enthusiastic smile. "Night, Mare. Drive carefully. Tell Clay hello."

"I will. I love you, Beth. And I think you're a wonderful friend." Maryann also hugged her, then scurried out the front door, her shoes tapping on the steps. "It's snowing again," she called before she tugged the door closed behind her.

"I hope Ronnie's okay. She was going out with some of the other kids. I hate it when it starts to snow and she's with a new driver. Anything could happen."

"Give it to God," Caitlin murmured, pulling open her own apartment door. "All of it." Her eyes twinkled with happiness. "It's surprising what wonderful things He can make out of our mistakes. Two of those surprises are right in there, waiting for me. If He did it for me, He can do it for you. Night, Bethy."

"Good night." Beth waited until Caitlin was inside before she walked back into her own apartment, her mind turning over all the things she'd shared tonight, things she'd kept bottled up for ten long years.

She tossed another log into the fireplace, poked it halfheartedly and then curled up in front of it, her back against the sofa.

"As if Garrett could still love me now," she muttered in disgust. "What a ridiculous idea! As if his father would let him, even if he were interested. Which he is not!" She shook her head in annoyance. "There's no point in even thinking about it, silly, because it just isn't going to happen."

The past hurts came back with a vengeance, and she suddenly wished she could go back to the security of life with Denis. "He was so kind," she muttered, remembering those blessed years of safety and sanctuary when she'd been able to probe her own thoughts and fears and begin dealing with them. "I did everything I could to make it work."

And it had worked. She and Denis had grown close, Ronnie had found friends, life had become full and busy. Beth had even taken a job at the local florist and learned, under Helen Smith's apt tutelage, how to make the most of every flower that came into her hands. In her spare time she'd taken all the courses she could. She'd filled her brain with all the things she'd once longed to study but hadn't had the funds or opportunity to tackle. And she'd fed her hungry heart with books, hundreds of them.

In the process, with Denis as her mentor, her bitter heart had healed there among the flowers in a place where ice and snow prevailed for much of the year.

"I'm older, hopefully smarter, and I can earn a living. I'm not a drain on society like Dad is. I can give Ronnie a home and maybe even veterinary school," she told the empty room. "I'm not that stupid needy child from the past."

She freely admitted that she'd been gullible back then. And a little too eager to avoid facing down anyone who seemed to have more than she did.

"If I had it to do again, I don't know whether I would take Charles Winthrop's advice or not. But then, maybe the girls are right—maybe I did need Denis and life with him to find out who I am."

The fire crackled and spit, and a glow of red danced on the walls. What was the best way to channel her energies now, outside work, to keep her mind off Garrett and the past? She spied the phone pad on a table nearby and stared at the scrawled message regarding a new youth center. Could she help?

*I can do this. I can't change the past, go back and explain everything to Gar. He wouldn't understand that scared little girl. But I can do this. I can make sure Ronnie and teenagers like her have a place to go where kids can mix and mingle freely without feeling out of place.*

She dialed the number slowly, thoughtfully.

"Renata? This is Beth Ainslow. No, I went back to my maiden name. Yes, it's good to hear your voice, too. It's about the youth center. I'd like to help." She scribbled down dates and times and nodded. "Sure. That's fine. I'll be there."

After they exchanged the latest news, Beth hung up and went back to her meditation by the fire.

Denis was such a good man. Why hadn't she kept his name? But it's time to face up to it. Inside I am an Ainslow, and it's time to face up to that. Denis would agree with that.

Wintergreen's front door opened, and the old oak floor squeaked as someone tiptoed across it. Beth held her breath as the lock in her own door turned and her sister slipped inside.

"Hi," she murmured quietly. "I was wondering where you were."

"Oh, you're still up. Good. We went out for coffee after youth group. Then I went back to Tyler's farm. Bethy, those horses!" Ronnie flopped down beside her sister and closed her eyes, blissfully sighing. "Someday I want to have horses like that, Beth. They're so beautiful."

"You were at the Winthrops'. Again." It wasn't a question. Beth felt her heart sink to her boots.

"Uh-huh. Garrett was there. He showed me around. It's a fantastic stable." She shifted, her face turning toward Beth. "Bethy, why didn't you ever tell me that you loved Garrett? And why did you marry Denis if you were in love with someone else? Do you still love Gar?"

Beth wilted.

Here was the question she'd avoided for ten long years. How could she possibly answer Ronnie when she didn't know the answer herself?

# Chapter Two

On Friday night Garrett punched the buzzer for Jordan and Caitlin's apartment and then stood back to admire Wintergreen. The old house loomed above him in the dark January evening like a specter from the past, even though there was nothing remotely ramshackle about it.

"Come on in, Garrett. You don't have to stand out here. You know that." Jordan thumped him on the back in a friendly manner, and held the door wide open. "Clay's here already. He's playing with my daughter because his isn't coming over for a while. Amy's at her figure skating lessons with some other children. Caitlin and Maryann are out, too."

Jordan motioned him in, then left the apartment door ajar. "Parts delivery," he explained. "I've got a monitor that keeps acting up."

Gar walked into the warm inviting apartment and admired the renovations. He'd only been here a couple of times lately, but the place intrigued him just the same.

"Have a seat."

"Clay." Gar nodded in greeting, accepted the mug of coffee from Jordan and took the big armchair. "You guys wanted to see me?" He didn't bother with social niceties. What was the point?

"Well, sort of. Though I've been meaning to ask you over for a while. Christmas and Clay's wedding sorta put the kibosh on my plans. We guys gotta stick together, you know." Jordan grinned but the glow didn't quite reach his eyes.

"We do?" Gar wondered at this sudden need for male bonding.

"We're thinking of forming a men's club." Clay handed the one-year-old Micah back to Jordan.

Gar hid his grin as he watched the farmer remove a glob of pureed peas from his shoulder. "A men's club? What for?"

"To give us something to do when it's ladies' night out!" Clay peered at him with a frown. "What do you do with all your spare evenings?"

"My parents are frequently away so I've been staying at their place, looking after Ty. That takes a lot of time."

"Looking after Ty?" Clay's bushy eyebrows rose. "He's almost eighteen, isn't he? How much looking after can he need?"

Gar grimaced. "You'd be surprised. He's been hanging out with that motorcycle gang that came to town last fall."

"Yeah, hanging out with them and Ronnie Ainslow!'' Jordan didn't pretend that wasn't the point of the whole conversation. ''She's nuts for those horses your parents keep.''

''I know. Ty's taken her riding lots of times. She's a natural, though Dad doesn't seem to like her coming out so much lately. Says he's afraid she'll get hurt, and he'll get sued.'' Gar leaned back to give the illusion he was relaxed. Truth to tell, he felt as if he were sitting on a crate of red-hot nails. These two wanted something from him. He just had to find out what.

''It's good, in a way. I mean, with her wanting to be a vet and everything.'' Jordan glanced up from his play with Micah. His golden eyes peered through the hank of hair that had fallen forward. ''Sure gonna be expensive to put her through that.''

Gar set his cup down and leaned forward, elbows resting on his knees, pretending a nonchalance he didn't feel. ''Okay, fellas. Why don't you just say what you want from me and we'll take it from there?'' he said quietly.

''Suits me.'' Clay glanced at Jordan, who nodded slightly. ''Money.''

''I beg your pardon?'' Gar frowned.

''I said, we're after money. Every year your family gives a big donation to the school to use for awards to the most promising student. It would be really nice if there were a scholarship this year for the student most likely to go into veterinary training.'' Clay shrugged. ''Or something like that. I'm not sure how they word it. Ty would probably know.

I guess you'd have to put a bug in the principal's ear.''

"And I would do this because…?'' Gar opened his eyes innocently wide.

"Because Ronnie Ainslow needs you to. There's no way Beth can afford a school like that—not with that little life insurance policy she got after Denis died. She most likely needs that to run her store.''

"How do you know about her finances?'' Gar glanced from one to the other, seeing the flicker of guilt on their transparent faces. "Who've you been talking to?''

"It's just that we were talking to Ty the other day,'' Clay sputtered finally, "when he came over to study with Ronnie. I was here delivering some of my furniture.'' He gulped. "Anyhow, he mentioned that Ronnie was real worried about asking Beth to help her choose a school. Apparently you have to start early.

"Anyway, Ty told us the fees are awful high. The girl's afraid her sister can't afford the school she wants, and she's thinking about changing her plans. We don't want to see that happen.''

So Ronnie and Ty had been discussing their future? Gar frowned as he wondered just how friendly the two actually were.

"And Ronnie's a natural with animals. She brought me in that dog that was hit last week, and it's perking right up.'' Clay cleared his throat. "You're the guy who knows all about compound interest and the value of investing early, aren't you? I'm sure if you run a spreadsheet analysis or something, you could see how valuable such a scholarship could be when she finishes school.''

Gar almost laughed. These two were suddenly worried about financial evaluations? It was ludicrous. He studied each of them for several moments. There was something behind this. Jordan didn't even bother to look away. He faced Gar head-on.

''Do it, Gar.'' Jordan's voice held no pretense. ''Do it because it's in your power and you'd do it for any other kid who showed so much promise. Because we asked you to.''

''And because you think I owe it to Beth. Is that it?'' The dawn of recognition hit Gar between the eyes. ''Because I didn't marry her and she's had such a hard life. I'm right, aren't I?''

Clay's mouth dropped onto his chest. He gulped once and then emitted a high-pitched squeak. ''Huh?''

Jordan wasn't nearly so delicate. ''If you feel that guilty, Bud, I guess it wouldn't hurt to offer a consolation prize.''

''I do not feel guilty.'' Gar strained to keep the even tone in his voice. ''She's the one who left, the one who married someone else.'' He swallowed. ''Anyway, it was ten years ago. Actually, eleven now. If I ever did feel any guilt, it's long gone.''

They were pushing this too far, shoving their noses in his business, Gar fumed silently. His relationship with Beth was private. Not that he had one at this point. Or expected to. It was just...

''You guys are making me nuts,'' he finally exploded.

"Sure, blame us. I didn't *say* you should feel guilty—did I, Clay?"

Clay obediently shook his head.

"No, of course I didn't." Jordan blinked innocently as he cuddled a sleepy Micah. "I was just suggesting something you might like to do for the good of the kids in the community, to help someone you know is having a tough time. You used to sort of like doing stuff like that. Remember Mrs. Carver?"

"Who?" Gar wondered if this happened to every man who got married. Neither Jordan nor Clay seemed able to keep the same thought in their heads for more than three minutes—it was very frustrating. "I don't know any Mrs. Carver. And what's that got to do with anything?"

"Yes, you know. The old woman who had that monstrously huge lawn at the end of Clagmore Drive. Every year she'd try to find someone to clean up those leaves, and every year all the kids in town were suddenly busy." Clay grinned. "Except you. You'd go out there and slave away for a whole Saturday just to earn a few bucks."

"Money was important to me. We had to earn our own, you know. My dad didn't believe in just doling it out." Gar shook his head. "What does this have to do with anything?"

"The point is, you didn't do it for the money, and we all knew that, Gar. You had a soft spot for the old girl." Jordan smiled sheepishly. "You've always been a giver."

"And, uh, Beth's finding it a little tight right now,

or so I heard.'' Clay coughed delicately behind one hand. ''January isn't the best month for the flower business. If her sister had a scholarship put away, say, even a small one to count on, that would take some of the pressure off. And then there's this summer camp. Ty showed me the brochure...'' His voice trailed away as he caught a glimpse of Gar's face.

It was pointless to argue with them. They were like a couple of old busybodies, arranging things behind everyone's back. Apparently they'd even sucked Ty into it. Garrett mentally calculated the amount left in the bank's budget for donations, and nodded.

''Fine. I'll ask the principal to have her fill out an application and bring it in to the bank.'' He surged to his feet. ''Is that all?''

''No.'' They said it in unison, glancing at each other in surprise.

Garrett exhaled, then sat back down, shifting uncomfortably under the intense scrutiny. ''Well?''

''The thing is,'' Clay began, ''we were kind of hoping this could be anonymous. You know, no strings attached.''

''I don't think Beth would let Ronnie accept anything from the bank, especially if she found out we were behind it.'' Jordan looked a little unnerved by the prospect. ''We, uh, sort of came by this information in a nonpublic way—if you know what I mean.''

He knew. Garrett sighed, wishing he'd had a board meeting or something urgent to attend tonight.

"Yeah, I know exactly how you got this information, Jordan. You eavesdropped, or else you pried it out of Ty." He glared at their unrepentant faces.

"I also know Beth wouldn't accept a plugged nickel from me. She doesn't care where I go, what I do, who I see or don't see. She's free and single and she doesn't have to answer to anyone." Gar forced the frustration out of his voice. "Thanks, guys, but I got the point the last time I had coffee and she happened by."

"It sounds to me like you're just a little too worried about what Beth Ainslow thinks. And if you ask me, you completely missed the point," Jordan grumbled, just low enough for Gar to hear.

"Actually, I didn't ask you, Jordan. But what, exactly, is the point? Don't tell me you two geniuses are setting yourselves up as matchmakers?" Gar glanced suspiciously from one to the other.

"Matchmakers? Who?" Jordan blinked.

"Us?" Clay squeaked, eyes innocently rounded behind his glasses. "No way."

"Because if you are," Gar went on, ignoring their studiously blank faces, "let me tell you that there is no point. The Beth Ainslow that lives across the hall from you, Jordan, is nothing like the Beth we knew in high school. She's cold and hard and determined to be the consummate businesswoman. She's not into the past. Not at all."

"Actually, according to our wives, she's exactly the same as she was then." Jordan set Micah down on the floor with a set of toy keys. "Caitlin says she's still hiding something that she won't share with anyone.''

"And Maryann says she's booking herself up with fund-raising for a community youth center so she won't have to stay home alone at nights." Clay winked at Jordan and then blinked in pretended surprise. "Hey, that's an idea! Why don't you get on the committee, too? Then you two could both work on the center. You are a member of the town council, Gar. It wouldn't be that hard to get yourself appointed.''

Gar frowned. "The community center? I haven't heard anything about her being on that board. I'm pretty sure I'm not sitting on it anyway.''

"You should pay more attention." Clay went to answer the door, and seconds later returned with his stepdaughter Amy. The little girl greeted everyone, then flopped down on the floor to play with the baby. "Our taxes pay you guys to keep your eyes peeled.''

You couldn't win with these two, Gar consoled himself. Just when you thought you had them beaten, they veered off the track onto something else.

"I'm on enough committees, I don't need any more." He ignored their fallen expressions. "I sure don't need to add any more meetings to my schedule. And the youth center idea is just getting off the ground. It'll mean hours of meetings.''

"You could do it for Ty's sake, couldn't you?" Jordan's smug grin made Gar nervous. "He'll benefit, too, you know.''

"How?"

"Instead of hanging around with the wildest crowd in town, he could be drawn in to the community center. Provided it was a cool—or hot—place to be. You know how kids are." Jordan winked at Clay. "If you can remember that far back."

"Cute, Andrews." Gar thought about it for a moment. "It could be mighty uncomfortable, you know. She's made it more than clear that I've been completely wiped from the slate of her mind."

"Well, what do you want her to say?" Clay rolled his eyes. *"Welcome home, darling"?* He snorted. "That's only in the movies, Garrett. Even I know that."

Gar sighed. Why had he come here? They reveled in embarrassing him, making fun of him and taunting him with these reminders of the past.

"Admit it, Gar. You still carry a torch for Beth. Maybe it's only flickering right now, but with a little fanning—"

"I do not carry any torch for Beth Ainslow! That was over long ago—the day she married someone else. I don't care about her one way or the other. So don't expect me to go kissing up to her now, because I have no reason to do that. She's the one who broke the engagement. She should apologize to me."

The words barely left his lips when a gasp of surprise alerted him.

Beth stood in the doorway, all five foot two of her diminutive frame bristling with anger. Her lips pursed together in a tight line as she glared at him. Her pint-size feet brought her to stand immediately in front of him.

Garrett turned and groaned, his whole body slumping with defeat. Talk about bad timing! He got to his feet slowly, knowing he'd said too much.

"I have nothing, *nothing,* to apologize to you for, Garrett Winthrop. But if it will make you feel better, I'm sorry I dumped you ten years ago. I thought, hoped, you'd be over it by now. There, feel better?" She wheeled around and stalked to the door, her strawberry-blond hair glittering in the lamplight.

Gar swallowed, remembering the hurt look in her eyes. He'd done that, without even meaning to. *Help me, God.*

Gar hadn't wanted to hurt her. He'd simply lashed out. He followed her to the door and laid one hand on her arm to stop her.

"Beth, I didn't mean to say that. I was just—"

She turned around, jerked her arm away from his touch and fixed him with her jade-green eyes.

"Just what? Spouting off? Angry? Still? Grow up, Garrett. This is a new era. We're adults now. It's time to move on." She glanced past him to Jordan. "I stopped by to tell you that Caitlin and Maryann will be delayed. They're discussing a Sweetheart's Banquet for sometime in February. Good night." Beth glanced at Gar, then turned and marched out of the room.

"Uh, thanks. Good night," Jordan called.

Gar turned and watched the other man's face as

the apartment door across the hall slammed shut. Jordan winced, his eyes squinting.

"Uh-oh." Clay, who'd risen moments ago, now flopped back down in his chair.

"Auntie Beth is mad," five-year-old Amy informed them all.

"No kidding! And it's all your fault." Gar scowled at the two men. "If you hadn't dragged me over here on some bogus excuse, I wouldn't now be the scum of the earth on Beth's shoes."

"It's not that bad." Jordan closed the door, apparently forgetting about his parts delivery as he returned to his seat. "She's just a little miffed."

"Yeah, right. And the Pacific is just a little pond." Gar stumbled over to an armchair and sank into it, thrusting his head into his hands. "Why do I get myself into these situations? I always end up the fall guy when I get near you two. When will I learn to shut up?"

"What you've got to do now is apologize." Clay grinned. "I've learned that much in my short marriage."

"How could I possibly apologize for saying she means nothing to me?" Gar stared dismally at the carpet.

"You weren't telling the truth, were you?" Jordan murmured, his eyes bright. "Because you actually care quite a bit for Beth Ainslow."

"He does?" Clay frowned. "But he said—" He stopped at the growling sound emanating from Jordan's throat. "Oh—" he nodded "—I get it."

"Gar?" Jordan was unrelenting.

"I don't know what I feel anymore." Gar raked a hand through his hair in frustration. "I loved her, you know. Really loved her. For years. I thought she felt the same, but then she just walked away. Without saying a word. It hurt."

"And now she's back." Jordan handed Amy a coloring book and a crayon from a box hidden inside the coffee table. "So?"

"What are you suggesting? That I try to pick up where we left off?" Gar made a face. "I'm not eighteen anymore."

"Uh-uh. You can never go back. If anybody knows that, it's us. Right, Clay?" Jordan didn't wait for a response. "What you need to do now is find out what you really want. I think you still care for her. That's why it hurts so much." He picked up Micah and cuddled her in his arms. "It's up to you, buddy. But I'll give you one piece of advice."

"Just exactly what I need. More of your advice." Gar rolled his eyes. "Okay, spout off. And then mind your own business."

Fortunately Jordan didn't take offense. "Forget the past. You can't change it, you can't make it go away. You can't alter her decision. She did what she did, and you don't know why. That's life. You might find out and you might not, but either way, it really doesn't affect the here and now. Deal with it and then decide what you want. If it's still Beth, go for it." He held Gar's gaze with his own for several moments, nodded and then walked over to the stairs with Micah.

"I've got to go change her. You guys are welcome to help yourselves to whatever you need." He climbed the stairs, murmuring sweet words of love to his daughter.

"Wow! He's been married—what? A little over a year? And he thinks he's an expert on everything." Gar sniffed as he lunged to his feet, showing Clay what he thought of Jordan's lately acquired perceptions. "I'm leaving." He buttoned up the coat he'd never removed and walked to the door. "See you, Clay."

"Gar?" Clay leaned down and whispered something to Amy, then walked toward him. "Can I say something?"

"Why not?" Resigned to hearing more than he'd ever wanted to on the subject of love, Gar stayed where he was.

"Jordan doesn't know everything, and sometimes his advice is a little off the wall. But in this case he's right." Clay jerked his head in the direction of Beth's apartment. "You need to let go of the past before it poisons the future. Maybe if you told her what was in your heart, you'd find out why she did what she did. Or maybe it wouldn't matter anymore."

Clay opened the door. "Either way, good luck, Gar."

"Luck? Ha!" Gar closed the door and stood in the hallway fuming. "If it weren't for bad luck, I wouldn't have any luck at all. Of all the lamebrain things to say."

Beth's door opened a crack and she peered out

above the chain, eyes narrowed. "Are you talking to yourself?"

"Actually, I was hoping to talk to you." He moved to stand in front of her door. "Just for a moment."

"I think you've said *everything* there is to say." She began to close the door. The emphasis on 'everything' couldn't be missed.

"Wait!" Gar thrust one loafer into the space and winced at the pressure against his toes. Given an opportunity, would Beth push even harder? "I really need to talk to you, Beth."

"No, you don't. You need to go home. And when you get there, send my sister home." She stood, waiting for him to remove his foot. "Well?"

Gar made up his mind. "You can let me in, and we'll talk in the privacy of your apartment, or I can stand out here and bellow for the whole world to hear. There are two very snoopy men across the hall who would relish relaying every word to their equally nosy wives. Your choice."

"Gar, be serious!"

But he'd made up his mind and he wasn't changing it. It was long past time they had this out. He, for one, needed a fresh start.

"I'm perfectly serious. Take your pick." He stayed exactly where he was, feeling the door press more tightly against his toes. "You have one minute to decide."

She glared at him for almost the entire time. But when he glanced at his watch and opened his mouth, she sighed, slid the chain off and opened the door.

"Fine. Have it your way, say what you want. Then we can close this chapter for good."

Gar walked inside, slid his scarf and gloves off and laid them over the back of a dilapidated rocker. *You just have to be firm,* he told himself proudly. *Insist on what you want.*

But wasn't that the problem? He didn't know what he wanted.

Not when it came to Beth Ainslow.

*I could use a hand here, God. Otherwise, I'm not going to be able to get both feet out of my mouth.*

# Chapter Three

"**W**ell?" Beth stood in front of the closed door, hands planted on her hips, and waited, her mouth a thin tight line.

"Do you have to be like that?" Gar ambled over to the sofa and gingerly sat down, wondering if the rickety old thing would hold him up. "I just want to talk. I'm not into whipping and public stoning anymore." It was a poor attempt at humor, and her eyes told him so.

She flounced over the worn carpet and sat down across from him, her legs curled like a pretzel beneath her.

"So talk."

"You're not being very nice," he chided. "It's just a conversation, Beth. I'm not going to threaten you or demand you explain anything."

She frowned at him, her green eyes pensive. Finally she let out her breath, a big sigh of resignation, and nodded. "Fine. I'll be as gracious as I can be under the circumstances."

"And what are these 'circumstances'?" he asked mildly. "We were engaged once, but we never got married. That's all."

"That's all?" She peered at him suspiciously. "Are you sure? That isn't what you said before. And you just told those two men that I mean nothing to you. I don't understand why you're here. Shouldn't you be accompanying Cynthia to something or other."

"Cynthia is just a friend," he muttered, his cheeks burning. "A close one, but only a friend." He sucked in a deep breath and let it out on a whoosh of truth. "The only woman I ever loved was you."

*Oh, God, please help me now!* he prayed seconds later as tears, big and fat, welled in her beautiful eyes.

"Don't cry, Beth. Please, don't cry." He felt as helpless as the newborn kittens Ronnie had helped their cat deliver last weekend.

"I'll cry if I want to," she sniffed, dashing the tears from her eyes. "I don't have to ask your permission."

She was so frustrating. That much hadn't changed. "Okay then, cry. I can't stop you." He sat there, feeling powerless and painfully belligerent and wondering why he'd decided to come in here tonight. Why hadn't he gone straight home and reamed out Ty for blabbing to his friends?

"Anyway, I'm not crying. I had something in my

eye." Beth's eyes still glimmered with the sheen of unshed tears. "Thank you for saying that."

"That I loved you?" He shrugged. "It's the truth. I accepted that a long time ago. I thought it was mutual." He avoided her gaze, tapping his toe against the worn Persian rug she'd laid in the living room. "I guess I had some growing up to do."

Beth didn't say anything, didn't offer an explanation, didn't even meet his glance when he finally looked up. Instead, she seemed to be studying the flames in the fireplace, a frown marring her smooth forehead.

"The thing is, I'm not sure where we stand now."

Her head jerked up at that. Gar barreled on. He needed to get this said. "I mean, are you mad at me for something? Did I do something you couldn't forgive? Should I get permanently lost?" He said everything but the one question that had plagued him for ten long years. *Did you really love me?*

He pretended not to study her as he peered over through his lashes. She straightened, drew a deep breath and stared directly at him. Gar held his breath, mentally preparing himself for what was to come.

"The problems I had in the past didn't really have to do with you, Gar. They had to do with me. With who I was and what I had to sort through. There have been many things I've had to deal with these past few years, but none of them were caused by anything you did."

"Why don't you just tell me?" he murmured, as

the words trembled on the edge of her lips. "I promise I'll listen."

Beth studied him for several tense moments, took a deep breath and plunged in. Gar forced himself to listen carefully to every word while studying her expressive face.

"When I was eighteen, I had this idea that marrying you would solve all my problems. Of course, you couldn't do that for me. Nobody could. Actually, it was a good thing that God led me away from Oakburn, where I could confront the real issues in my life."

Gar frowned. "God led you away? How do you figure that?"

He didn't get any of this. There was something she was trying to tell him.

"There are some things I probably should have told you years ago," she murmured. "Things that would have explained some of how I acted. I think the time has come to tell you now. If you want to hear them."

"Yes, of course. But we knew each other pretty well, Beth. I don't think there's much you can say that I don't already know about you." He saw her grimace, and hastily backtracked. "I'll listen to anything you have to say."

"Do you remember that Easter sunrise service we had that year? The one where we dedicated our lives to serving God, to knowing Him as a real Father?" She waited for his nod. "I had the wrong idea of a father then, Gar. I didn't understand what God the

Father meant, and when I thought about it, the only picture I ever got was my dad.''

"And?'' He waited for her to continue, watching as her fingers fiddled with the fringe on the scarf she wore.

"Did you ever meet my dad?''

He frowned. "Yeah, a couple of times, I guess. When we were dating, he was away a lot. I figured he was some kind of workaholic. After college, well, I was busy. I only saw him once in a while.'' He waited for some comment, but it never came. Instead, Beth seemed intent on her next words.

"My father was as far from the ideal father as you could get. After Mom died, he couldn't seem to dig himself out of his depression. I think Ronnie and I reminded him of what he'd lost, and that's why he drank so much.''

Drank *so much?* "Your father always seemed fine to me. Sure, he drank a little, but he had it under control. Didn't he?''

She shook her head, her eyes clear.

"No, he didn't. Oh, he always had a good reason for anyone who cared to ask, but the truth was that he had a serious problem and it affected our home. Everything I did revolved around that problem and how it impacted on Ronnie and me. It wasn't a pleasant life.''

"Were you in danger?'' he asked, anger surging through his veins.

"No. He'd generally disappear until he was sober again. And if you let him ease back into the routine without comment, he was fine.'' She met his gaze.

"I couldn't tell you, Gar. I was too embarrassed. I figured you'd realize how totally unsuitable I was to be going out with you. That's why I never asked you to come to my house. I know you must have wondered."

Gar figured that for someone the rest of the town considered a relatively smart man, he was incredibly dense. "Actually, I never really noticed. Ronnie was with us, so I guess I just accepted that you had to care for her. Anyway, there was always lots of room at our place, and my dad liked to keep an eye on us."

How well he remembered those intensely scrutinizing eyes.

"Yes, I did have to watch Ronnie. I was more of a mother to her than a sister."

Gar noticed that she avoided mentioning her father. For some reason he'd never understood but intuitively known, the two of them had never really gotten along. Was his drinking the reason?

"And Ronnie was the reason you left here? Married Denis?" he prodded, watching the array of emotions fly across her face.

"Sort of." He saw her draw a lungful of air. "After you went away to college, I was alone a lot. I couldn't find a permanent job, Dad got laid off, and Ronnie and I had nothing in the house, sometimes for days, when Dad would disappear after a bender."

He wondered how dearly it had cost her to say that. Knowing Beth's pride, Gar figured it wasn't easy to reveal how desperately hard up they'd been.

"Surely there was someone who could have helped. The church or a social agency?" He saw her lips tighten and knew it was a stupid thing to say. Someone should have noticed without being told.

"I suppose if they'd known, they would have," she agreed dully. "But I didn't want anyone to know how awful it was." She smiled sadly. "Pride. Silly irresponsible pride that meant Ronnie went without when she didn't have to." Beth shook her head. "I'll never forgive myself for that."

"And you left because…?"

"I left because I had to get a job in a place where I could earn some money and provide for both of us. We were destitute. I couldn't live like that anymore, and I wouldn't let Ronnie stay home alone, with *him*. After a lot of heart-searching and debate, I became convinced that leaving was the only thing to do. By then I knew I wasn't going to marry you. You needed someone more your equal. I borrowed some money to start out, and left to try and start over." Her voice trailed away.

Gar glanced up and saw a flash of pain enter and leave her eyes. She was still hiding something— something she wasn't ready to tell him. Should he ask?

As he watched those delicate narrow shoulders bow under the strain of a memory that obviously still stung, Gar knew he wouldn't probe farther. He'd seen the shame on her face, and knew that she hated talking about those days. He wasn't too crazy about rehashing them, either. Wasn't it better to let it all go, and see what could happen from hereon?

"I'm glad you told me." He stayed where he was, watching as she drew herself erect, her dignity draped like a cloak around her. "And that's why you wanted to see me that weekend? To tell me you were going away?"

She nodded. "I owed you that. I didn't want to send a letter. I thought it was something I needed to do in person. I wanted to tell you to get on with your life, not to worry about us. Eventually, though, I had to write it. It was the hardest thing I've ever done."

*A letter?* Gar frowned. He'd never gotten a letter from her. But then, maybe she hadn't mailed it. After all, it couldn't have been easy for an eighteen-year-old girl to uproot herself from everything familiar, and, with little sister in tow, take off for parts unknown. He'd ask about it later.

"I'm sorry, Beth. If I had known, I'd have done everything I could to get back here and help you out. You should have told me." He felt the old anger rise and shoved it down with resolution. Jordan was right. There was no profit in rehashing what could have been.

"I've been reminded many times lately that all of that is in the past. And this is the present. So where do we go from here?"

He held his breath, waiting for her answer. And as he did, he prayed that it wouldn't hurt too much when she told him she hated him.

"I don't know. There are so many things to think about." She smiled tremulously. "I don't want to make any more decisions right now, Gar. It was hard enough to come back here when Ronnie decided she had to meet Dad. Now, I just want to relax and take one day at a time—see what God has in store for me. I want to focus on business and prove to the world that Beth Ainslow isn't a total write-off. Is that okay?''

''I'm sure nobody ever thought that you were a write-off, Beth,'' he offered, seeing the glint of tears return to those vivid green eyes. ''What about me? Will it bother you that I'm around Wintergreen to pick up Ty? He seems to home in on this place after school.''

''No,'' she said firmly, her clear gaze meeting his. ''I'm glad Ronnie's found a friend, and I'm glad it's Ty. We can't go back to what we had, but maybe we can still be friends. Someday. If you can put the past behind you, I can, too. You're welcome here anytime, Garrett.''

He pressed home his advantage. ''And if I asked you out?''

Beth shook her head. ''I don't think that's a good idea, Gar. Not with everyone already speculating about you and Cynthia, and probably me, too. Right now, what I really need is a friend.''

''Then you've got one.'' He stood, once more buttoning the coat he'd never removed. Beth stood, too, peering up at him, her bare feet reducing her height considerably from the heels she usually wore.

''Thank you,'' she murmured, holding out her hand.

Gar took it, heart thumping as her smooth alabaster palm lay warmly against his. ''If you need anything, anything," he repeated, "promise you'll let me know."

"Oh, you'll know." She grinned and self-consciously pulled her hand away. "Probably before the week's out. I'm going to apply for a loan."

He liked that impish gleam that sparkled deep in her eyes. It reminded him of happier times. "I just happen to know the boss," he quipped. "I'll put in a good word for you."

Her smile immediately fell away, but she hid it, walking in front of him to pull open the door.

"Thanks for talking to me, Gar. I was kind of dreading this confrontation, but you've made it much easier for me."

"I'm glad." He didn't know what else to say, so he bid her good-night and left the old house, her earlier words still ringing in his ears.

*Ronnie and I had nothing in the house, sometimes for days.*

How did I miss it? Why didn't I see something, anything? he wondered as he drove to his parents' house.

"Well, Garrett, where have you been all this time? Your mother and I ate long ago. We were hoping you'd be here." His father stood in the marbled entry, his eyes probing. "Some secret assignation? Cynthia called three times."

Gar frowned. "Why would you think I was meeting someone secretly?" he asked as he hung up his coat.

A look of something—relief perhaps—flickered in his father's eyes. "Just a joke. I'm having a second cup of coffee in the den if you want to join me. That Cynthia is a real nice girl. Well-mannered. Her family is from good stock. Is she someone special?''

Gar trailed along behind into the elegantly appointed oak-lined den his father had inhabited for years. But his mind whirled with what he'd just heard.

"We're just friends. Dad, what do you know about Mervyn Ainslow?''

His father's nimble fingers hesitated just a moment before they poured out two cups of coffee from the silver coffeepot. He added cream and sugar to his own before passing Gar a cup of black.

"Ainslow? Oh, you mean Ronnie's father.'' Charles Winthrop sank back into his tufted leather chair and sipped his coffee. "Not a lot. As I recall, the man had a drinking problem. At least, that's what I heard years ago.''

"And the church deacons didn't offer to do anything for him, or for the girls? Especially with their mother gone?''

His father glanced up warily. "Why would you ask that? Is the man in trouble or something?''

"No. He's in a nursing home right now. I was just wondering how Ronnie and Beth had made it through back then. Nobody in this entire town seems to have lifted even their pinky to make sure the kids were okay.'' He stared at Charles, waiting for his denial. To his surprise, there was none.

"I'm afraid we're guilty there, son. Most of us just didn't want to see how bad Merv really was.

He missed Loretta terribly, I suppose. Just as I would miss your mother.''

''Sometimes they had no food.'' For some reason Gar felt inclined to push the issue. He wondered at the sudden whiteness of his father's face. ''Are you all right?''

''Certainly. Just a little indigestion.'' His father buried his nose inside his cup, only to jerk it out moments later. ''Why bring all this up now?'' he demanded.

''I was talking to Beth tonight. She told me a little about why she left town ten years ago.''

Charles surged to his feet and hurried over to replace his cup on the tray. With his back turned toward his son he asked, ''Did she call you—ask you to go there?''

''No. I was at Wintergreen to meet with Jordan and Clay.'' He frowned, watching as his father fiddled with the cream pitcher. ''Is everything really all right, Dad?''

''Certainly. Fine. Perfect. Think I'll go talk to your mother for a while.'' Charles stalked across the room and pulled open the door. ''That young girl is here again,'' he muttered. ''I'm not sure it's a good thing for Ty to be hanging around with her so much. He forgets his responsibilities.''

Gar followed his father down the hallway and watched as he began to climb the stairs.

''Why shouldn't she come around if she wants to?'' he demanded, frowning. ''Ronnie's a perfectly fine girl, and she might even help Ty get his grades up. He should be looking for a college soon, you know."

His father quickened his pace. "She's not our kind, son. Childhood friends are one thing, but the boy needs to think about the future. So do you. See you later."

"Yeah, see you," Gar muttered, then added to himself, "What did I say wrong this time—?"

"He does that all the time. Talks to himself, I mean. I think it's a big brother thing. Or maybe senility."

Gar whirled around to see Ty and Ronnie standing behind him, huge grins spread across their faces. Apparently they hadn't heard his father's last remarks.

"Hi, you two. What are you doing?"

"Looking for something to eat. We missed dinner."

Ty didn't look worried in the least, and Gar couldn't help but smile. In the old days he'd gone out of his way to make sure he was on time for meals. Tardiness meant a long-winded lecture—and he'd hated those. Apparently Ty wasn't as concerned.

"I guessed you'd be here with the old folks." Scorn laced through Ty's squeaky voice. "You gotta get a life, Gar."

"For your information," Garrett enunciated, leading the way to the kitchen, "I was out. And I'm starved, too. I missed dinner."

"Boy, you're really living it up!" Ty shoved his way in front of Garrett and yanked open the fridge.

"Cook left some sliced chicken, some kinda salad stuff and—wow!—lemon pie." He pulled everything out as he spoke and piled it on the counter. "Come on, Ronnie. Let's eat."

Gar whisked away a slice of the pie before his brother appropriated it all, helped himself to several slices of chicken and a healthy portion of the Caesar salad after Ronnie had chosen barely enough to feed a mouse.

"You eat even less than your sister used to," he remarked, smiling at her as he offered a can of soda. "I think she got more carryout containers than anyone else in town back in those days." The reason for that suddenly hit him, and he gulped. How could he have been so stupid as not to have seen why?

"Beth's never eaten much," Ronnie murmured, shaking her head at Ty's offer of pickles. "But she's crazy for sweets. I gave her this huge chocolate Santa for Christmas, and it was gone before noon." She giggled. "We had a great time."

Gar remembered his Christmas at Aspen, and suddenly wished he'd stayed home. He'd been trying to avoid her after Maryann and Clayton's wedding, but she'd stayed in his mind so effectively that he might as well have planted himself at Wintergreen in the front hall and watched Beth come and go. Instead, he'd spent New Year's wondering who she was celebrating with.

"Just ignore him," he heard Ty mutter around a mouthful of food. "He's kinda spaced." He bounded up from his stool at the counter and snapped two fingers in front of Gar's face. "Yo, earth to Gar. Anybody home?"

Gar sighed. No respect, that was the problem. Everyone else seemed to think he was worthy of it—everyone except his own kid brother. "What is it, Ty?"

"I asked where you were that you had to miss dinner?" Ty rolled his eyes at Ronnie before returning to his seat. "I figured you'd be eating out with good ol' Cynth. She's kinda dull, like you."

"Cynthia Reardon?" Ronnie's eyes widened. "She's gorgeous, Ty. So elegant and refined. I wish I was more like her. Instead I'm plain."

"No, you're not," Ty replied. "You're good-looking in a different kind of way. And you know how to have fun. Cynthia's as stiff as cardboard. 'Good evening, Mr. Winthrop,'" he mimicked in a falsetto. "'Thank you so much for inviting me over to your ball. I just adore those sculptures.' Yuk!" He shuddered.

"Ty, that's unkind and totally untrue. Cynthia is very bright, and a kind woman besides. She's certainly forgiven you for any number of faux pas." Gar placed his dishes in the dishwasher and turned to face his brother. "But, for your information, Cynthia and I are just friends."

"Does she know that?" Ty's eyes dared him to answer that. "She's looking for more than friendship."

"Well, that's all I'm offering." He ignored his brother's snort of derision and turned to Ronnie. "I'll drive you home, when you're ready."

"Thanks." She smiled, putting her own dishes away. "But I don't want to put you out. Beth said she'd come and get me."

"Your sister has been working all day. Why don't we give her a break. You call and tell her I'll drop you off, okay?" He waited for her nod and then glanced at Ty. "I'm going up to change, and then we can go. Try and get your homework finished, will you, Ty?"

"Nag, nag, nag." Ty's mouth turned down. "The parents already have one golden boy, why do they need another one? I'm not cut out for bank stuff, Gar. I want to do something else."

"Like what?" Gar stopped where he was, frowning as he undid his tie.

"I'm not saying. You'll just tell me how dumb it is." Ty turned back to Ronnie, a dejected set to his thin shoulders. "Come on, Ron. Let's go get your stuff. It was fun riding through the woods, wasn't it?"

"It was wonderful! You're so lucky to live here." Ronnie waved at the huge expanse of snow-covered lawn that stretched out beyond the patio doors in the dining room. "You can have all the pets you want without bothering anyone."

Gar left them there, chattering, as he headed up to his room. He caught the tail end of Ty's complaints.

"Yeah, but you've got the real freedom," his brother murmured. "You don't have to fit a mold. You can be anybody you want. That's way better."

Gar thought about that as he changed into jeans

and a sweatshirt. Was Ty really so unhappy with his life? He himself had never minded school, had reveled in the academic subjects and had made the team in three sports. Tyler seemed to have none of those interests. Gar wondered why that was. Was he missing something there, too, just as he'd missed Beth's problems.

He vowed to pay more attention. And he'd speak to his father about having Ronnie out more often. Despite his father's worries, Gar was certain that Veronica Ainslow was a great influence on Ty. And driving her home gave him another connection with Beth.

That was good.

Wasn't it?

# Chapter Four

A week after her meeting with Gar, Beth forced her fingers to unclench. Then she pushed the glass paneled door of the bank open and resolutely stepped inside. The most expensive building in town bustled with activity, yet still managed to gleam with buffed elegance. The brass railings and glass partitions shone, totally free of grubby fingerprints and dust.

"I wonder if their cleaners do houses," she muttered to herself as she walked steadily past the tellers to the loans department. Yeah, right. Like Winthrop's cleaners would touch her dinky apartment.

"Hi, Beth. Chilly one today, isn't it?" Glynis Johnson smiled from behind her big oak desk. "Need those thermal things these days."

"Don't I know it." Beth pulled off her gloves, hoping she looked businesslike. "I had to refuse a shipment of long stems this morning. They were frozen solid.''

"Oh, poor things! I don't know how you can stand to see those beauties ruined like that.'' Glynis pulled a sheaf of papers from the top basket of her desk. "Now, I suppose you'd like to get through this as quickly as possible. No businesswoman I know wants to be away from work when the door is open.''

"Thanks, Glynis. I appreciate your help, and the way you've kept this quiet. I know this town is like a bubble where everyone knows everyone else's business, but I really don't want this to get around. Not just yet, anyway.'' She took the folder full of papers and opened it, gulping at the myriad rows and columns that confronted her.

"Don't pass out! It looks like a lot, but it's not really that bad. We just like to have a bit of history to base our decisions on. If you need help, I could take a few minutes and show you—''

"Thanks, Glynis, but it's all right. I filled out all those forms before I ever opened the Enchanted Florist. I can handle these.'' She glanced around. "Is there someplace I can sit?''

"Sure, use this office. It's empty at the moment.'' Glynis opened a door to her left and indicated the empty desk and chair. "If you need help, just yell. I've got a pretty light day.''

"Thanks. You're very kind.''

"Not at all. Things always slow down when Gar goes out of town. But he always brings back twenty times more work for me, so I don't feel bad about relaxing once in a while.'' She grinned and pulled the door almost closed behind her.

So Garrett wasn't in the bank today? Good. That made it easier to do this. She laid out the sheets, took a deep breath and concentrated on the first one. She could do this. She had to do this. Ronnie was counting on her.

Twenty minutes later, voices disturbed her.

"I'm sorry, Mr. Winthrop. I didn't know you had asked the Thomms to come in today. I'm sure the office will be free in a moment."

Beth jerked to attention, then quickly shoved the sheaf of documents inside the folder. "It's all right, Glynis. I'm finished anyway." She stood, eyes trained on the door. "Hello, Mr. Winthrop."

The elder Winthrop stared at her, his eyes chilly. Finally he responded. "Miss, er, Mrs.—" He stopped. "I'm sorry, I don't know how to address you."

She was fairly certain the remark was supposed to make her cower, but she refused to be put down. She had a perfectly good reason for being here. "Beth," she enunciated clearly. "Beth Ainslow. Surely you remember?"

"Beth has an appointment to talk to you in—" Glynis consulted her watch then smiled at them both, "—in two minutes." She reached for the folder. "All finished with these?"

"I've done as much as I'm going to. I think the *pertinent* information is all there." She ignored the frowning look Glynis gave her. "Is Mr. Winthrop free now?"

"Uh, yes. That is, I believe so. If you'll come this way, I'll let the Thomms in here." She led Beth out of the office and to an etched-glass door with the name and title Charles Winthrop, President embossed on the frosted pane. "Have a seat, Beth. I'm sure he'll be with you shortly."

Beth sat because her legs wouldn't allow her to stand any longer. The room had been redecorated since the last time she'd been here, but the walls were still warm with the mahogany paneling. Under her feet, the carpet was the thickest broadloom she'd ever seen, it's brilliant jade color rich against the wood.

"I can't do this," she decided, and gulped nervously as she eyed the expensive brass fixtures lying neatly on the desk. Who used a brass letter opener these days?

Nothing had changed. She didn't fit in here any more now than she had then. What did she know about mortgages and profit-and-loss sheets? Who was she to be in here, bearding the lion in his den?

"Miss Ainslow, I have no idea why you need to see me privately. I don't believe we have anything to say to each other." Charles Winthrop strode across the room, seated himself behind his desk and folded his hands on top of the immaculate blotter. "Do we?"

"Uh, well, that is—" Beth heard herself stammering and felt a heat wash over her cheeks. Nothing had changed. Nothing! She was still intimidated by this man and his wealth. She had nothing, she was a nobody. And he was rich and well-known, needing nobody, nothing and no one.

"Yes, Miss Ainslow? Why did you ask to see me?"

Something in his tone, some underlying note of concern made her look up. She studied his face—leaner, lined with worry, drawn tight even though he'd apparently just returned from a skiing holiday. And something inside her clicked.

Charles Winthrop was a businessman. He earned his money by using other people's money. He would loan her money and charge her an exorbitant amount for that. It was a business arrangement. But that's all it was. There was no hidden hierarchy. No more than there was when a customer came in to her shop hoping to do some business.

She straightened in her seat, shoulders back, chin up. She was an equal here, a businesswoman prepared to offer him an opportunity, not some lowly eighteen-year-old filled with self-doubts.

"I'm here to enquire about a loan from your bank, Mr. Winthrop. I'd like to purchase a building that I've learned will be going up for sale. My present location is far too small to generate the kind of sales I am currently projecting and achieving." She took a deep breath and waited for his response.

"Well." Charles Winthrop folded and refolded his hands, chagrin contorting the patrician lines of his face. "I see." He recovered quickly. "We must have some information before we grant loans, Ms. Ainslow."

Beth smiled, noting that he'd settled for her

maiden name, but attached the "Ms." lest anyone misconstrue her as single.

"I've given Beth the forms and I believe she's completed them, Mr. Winthrop." Glynis edged through the door, carrying a tray with two cups of steaming coffee. "I thought you might like your coffee while you discuss this."

She seemed totally unaware of the tense atmosphere that hung between the other two, but went quietly about handing out the cups and offering cream and sugar, then glided back out the door. Beth took a sip for fortification.

"I believe you'll find what you need in here," she murmured, handing across the file folder with its contents.

He took it, set it on his desk and then peered across at her. "Are you sure there isn't someone you'd like to consult first? Perhaps someone with a bit more, er, experience in such matters? A new business is generally on rather tenuous ground until it has proved itself for a period of time."

Beth nodded. "Yes, generally speaking I'd agree with you. Except when that business is suffering because it cannot grow any more under the present circumstances." She sat back and folded her hands in her lap.

"Thank you, but I don't need to speak to anyone, Mr. Winthrop. My degree has given me some knowledge in this matter, and I feel confident I can handle the purchase myself, with my lawyer's advice, of course." She took a deep breath of confidence. She wasn't that insecure little girl from ten years ago. She was a businesswoman, and she needed this loan if she hoped to expand and build up business enough to support Ronnie when she left for college.

"As you may be aware, I am now renting. I'm obligated only by the month. I can give notice at any time, and it seems to me that January would be a good opportunity to do that. Once we are a little closer to Valentine's Day, I'll be receiving larger shipments and I'll need the additional area for arranging displays."

He nodded. "Yes, I can see how the extra space could be valuable. But surely that space isn't income-generating. It's work space. Perhaps if you worked later at night, or came in earlier..." His voice trailed away. "I'm sorry, perhaps you are already doing that."

It sounded smug and overbearing. But maybe it wasn't a put-down, Beth considered. Maybe he was just trying to be sure she'd considered other options. Well, she had. And thoroughly. But no matter how much she shifted and reorganized and rearranged, there simply was not enough room. She knew that— now it was up to her to convince him of it.

"Yes, I have. We worked in triple shifts through the Christmas season to accommodate our customers as best we could, but I'm afraid there are still unexpected funerals and walk-in customers who don't want to pick something up tomorrow or the day after. We simply must have more room." She held her temper in check and calmly listed the reasons for her decision.

To his credit, Charles Winthrop listened to her plans for expansion into Belgian chocolates and the ever-popular stuffed animals. He nodded when she spoke about the market in items other than fresh flowers, and she couldn't help but feel a warm glow at his obvious surprise. She'd done her homework, and done it well.

"So, as you can see, this isn't some fly-by-night idea of mine. I intend to stay in Oakburn and make this business grow strong and healthy." She held his gaze, never wavering under the intense scrutiny.

"And your plans for the future?" His voice hinted at something.

"My sister would like to go to veterinary college when she's finished high school. That will be fairly costly, but if at all possible, I'd like to send her. That's why I want to get things going on the right foot at my store." If he was asking about Gar, Charles Winthrop was going to have to come right out and ask her.

"I see. You plan to stay at your current home, then? Continue to pay rent at that house— What's it called?"

"Wintergreen." She frowned. "Caitlin has been very kind. And yes, the apartment suits me quite well. Ronnie is near the school and there is always someone around."

"And your father?"

The softly voiced enquiry made her sit up straighter, sent her shoulders back.

"I'm sure you're aware my father is in the local nursing home where he is being taken care of. He has all he needs there. I am not responsible for him financially, if that's what you're asking.'' She swallowed the rest of the words. This wasn't the time to defend a man who had no defense, even if she wanted to. She needed this loan.

''Why did you come back?'' The question seemed forced, as if he hadn't wanted to ask it but couldn't help himself.

Beth shifted uncomfortably. ''Ronnie wanted to see Dad again. She doesn't have much memory of him, and she wanted to fill in the gaps before it was too late.''

''Perhaps it's better that she doesn't. I understand from my son that he was absent quite frequently.''

The well-polished scorn in those tones sent her hackles up, and for the first time in her life Beth defended the man she'd been sure she hated.

''My father loved my mother. When she died, he couldn't get past his grief. Yes, he drank. Too much. And yes, I suppose you even know that he left us alone for days on end. When he was home, he did the best he could. Perhaps that's the most anyone can do.'' She glared at him, daring him to say more.

Long minutes passed as he sat there, ensconced behind his elegant desk, studying her from behind his gold-rimmed glasses. She couldn't read his face. He'd had too much practice hiding his emotions. Nothing much had changed there.

Beth was fed up with the whole event. Certain that it was pointless to continue, and needing desperately to get away from this cloying atmosphere, Beth gathered up her purse and coat.

"Thank you for your time, Mr. Winthrop, but I have to get back to work. I'll leave those papers with you. I'm sure you'll need some time to decide." Actually, he'd probably already decided. And no doubt the answer would be a resounding "no." At least she'd tried.

She pulled open the door to his office, looking back over her shoulder as she did. "Please have Glynis phone me as soon as you've made your decision. I'd like to get moving immediately, if possible. As you already know, I always pay back my loans."

She nodded and then stepped through the door, careening into a solid mass almost twice her size.

"Beth?" Strong lean hands held her steady as she caught her breath. "What are you doing here?"

"Gar." She pulled herself away, mentally aware of the fresh lime tang of his cologne—he still used the same one. "Talking to the president of this bank. Excuse me, please."

Beth moved past him and down the glossy floor in a straight beeline for the door. She did not want to be there when Garrett discussed her loan application with his father. And he would. As a member of the board, a registered financial consultant and second in command, Gar's opinion would be sought.

Once outside, she breathed in the cold, crisp air and glanced up at the bright blue winter sky. Whatever happened, she'd done her best. It was in God's hands now.

Back at the shop her part-time helper was busy explaining the variety of cut flowers that could be assembled on such short notice. Beth checked the messages lying by the phone and frowned. The nursing home? What did they want?

She dialed the number. "This is Beth Ainslow. I understand someone called me."

She listened as the voice on the other end of the line explained that the home was having a potluck supper for the families. "I have your note here and just wanted to be sure you are aware of this opportunity to spend time with your loved one."

My note? Beth peered out the huge plate-glass window and groaned as enlightenment dawned. Ronnie! It had to be. She was so determined to get to know her father.

"And this is tonight?" Beth nodded, her voice quiet. "Thank you for phoning. Goodbye."

She had no doubt that Ronnie knew all about the supper. She'd been to the nursing home many times, and except for Christmas Day, all without Beth. There were notes plastered all over the fridge at home about upcoming events.

Beth knew she'd have to go. If she kept on avoiding her father, the whole town would begin speculating as to what had happened in the Ainslow household. Next would come a debate on why she'd *really* left town.

"He's old, he's half senile, he can't hurt us anymore." But even as she recited the words, Beth knew it wasn't the present she feared as much as the resurfacing of the past.

"She's applying for a loan? Why?" Gar listened as his father explained, running over the figures she'd neatly printed on the forms he held. "Expanding already, huh? Good for her. You'll approve it, of course."

"Approve it?" His father glared at him. "Have you lost all your sense, Garrett? She has very little collateral, almost no assets, and her ideas are risky."

"I think they're very sound and she's proven them by the looks of these statements. She's good at what she does, Dad. Why not give her a chance? That's how Grandpa started this place, remember?" Gar watched the fine pink flush rise from his father's collar.

"That was a long time ago. People didn't default on their debts then like they do now." Charles straightened the immaculate piles of paper on his desk, then glanced up. "I recommend we refuse."

"Then I'll stand as guarantor myself." Gar met his father's startled glance. "She deserves a chance, Dad. And she's not going to default. If that business fails, it won't be because Beth hasn't put every single ounce of effort she has into making it a go."

"You don't feel obligated, or something, do you? I mean, it was just a silly, childish crush that the two of you shared in school. You were both too young to know better. You've moved past that with Cynthia."

Gar shook his head. "Cynthia and I are just friends. How many times have I told you that, Dad? And I'm not so sure my feelings for Beth are in the past. I didn't have a 'crush' on her, I was in love with her. And she loved me."

Charles sprang to his feet, his eyes blazing. "What do you mean, son? It was over years ago. She ran out on you."

"She left Oakburn to get a job so she could support her sister and herself." Gar stared at his father's angry face. "Why does all this bother you so much, Dad?"

"She's been married, Gar. *Married!*" Charles flopped back down in his elegantly tufted chair. "How could this girl have loved you if she married someone else?"

It was a question Gar had asked himself a hundred times. And he'd never found an answer. Wasn't it funny that now one came immediately to mind.

"She was alone, with a child to support. I'm sure Denis Hernsley was a nice man and his, uh, support would have been appreciated." He couldn't make himself say the word *love*.

"Exactly! If she loved you, why didn't she come to you? Why go to him? She must have loved him, don't you think?"

Gar shook his head vehemently. "No, I don't think that at all, Dad. I think she was a mixed-up kid who couldn't handle her life here and tried to do the best she could somewhere else. And I think it's up to us to see to it that she gets a fair shake in this town. We owe her that much, don't you think?" He frowned as his father's face blanched.

"W-what do you mean, Gar?"

"I mean that someone in this town should have seen what those two were going through ten years ago. Somebody should have reached out a hand of hope and helped them. And I'm one of those people. I was engaged to the woman, and I didn't see what was right in front of my face."

"It wasn't your fault, Garrett. You were just a kid. It wasn't mine, either." Charles wiped his pristine white handkerchief across his forehead. "Mervyn Ainslow is a drunk. Nobody but him can change that."

"I'm not debating that, Dad." Why was the old man getting so hot under the collar? It was as if he knew something no one else knew. Gar shook his head. How ridiculous. "All I'm saying is that those two girls should have been able to count on the church, the community, someone. Oakburn goofed up back then, Dad. But we're not going to make that mistake again. Are we?"

He fixed his father with a stern look that dared him to deny Beth the opportunity to make good. If worse came to worst, he would invoke his grandmother's help, plead for her to insist on helping someone who deserved a chance.

"Well?"

Charles sighed and signed his name to the bottom of the application. "Very well, she can have the loan. But the bank will assume the risk. I won't have you tying yourself up with someone else's problems for the next ten years." He thrust the papers at Gar. "Besides, I thought you were advising the Forsyths to hang onto that property. Now, suddenly you want them to sell?"

Gar ignored the jibe, shuffling all the paperwork for Beth's loan into a neat pile.

"As someone recently pointed out to me, the Forsyths are retired and their biggest dream is to travel. Why should they have that building hanging around their necks the whole time? The cash from this sale will give them a lot more enjoyment than that pile of brick and mortar."

Charles sniffed. "Miss Ainslow's advice, no doubt?"

"As a matter of fact, it was. That's one thing you have to admit, Dad. Beth has her head on straight." He grinned at his father's dubious look. "I'll go tell her."

Charles mumbled something like "straight to the money," but Gar ignored him and left the office. On his way out he hugged Glynis so close that her feet left the floor. The woman gave a shriek of dismay and then giggled with delight as he set her down.

"Mr. Garrett, you shouldn't be doing that to an old woman like me. I could have heart failure!" She straightened her prim white blouse and long black skirt.

Gar burst out laughing, his knuckles brushing her talcum-scented cheeks. "Never, Glynis. You're much too young and healthy." She preened before his eyes, and he strode across to his own office, grinning from ear to ear.

It took two seconds to dial the number he'd memorized months ago. "Beth, it's me, Garrett. Your loan has been approved. We can go ahead with the paperwork right away, if you'd like." He listened to her shocked silence and then her burst of questions. "Dad makes up his own mind. But we'd be fools if we didn't look to the future with an eye to keeping Oakburn growing, now wouldn't we?''

She agreed, her voice breathless with relief. He could almost see those blue eyes soften and lighten.

"How about coming out for dinner tonight? To celebrate?''

"I can't, Gar. But thanks for asking." Her voice immediately changed, grew harsh and cold.

"Oh.'' He swallowed down his disappointment. "I'm sorry, Beth. I didn't mean to take anything for granted.''

"It's not that. Ronnie's arranged for us to attend a potluck at the nursing home. I-I think I'd better go.''

He knew how hard it would be for her to go there and pretend that she was glad to visit her father. Somehow he felt sure that when Beth looked at her father, she remembered the past, and the bitterness of it welled up inside all over again. She'd talked of moving on, but she would have to deal with those feelings first.

"I'm sorry," she whispered, a catch in her voice. "Maybe another time.''

"Nah, I think tonight is as good a time as any.'' He made some swift calculations. "I'll pick you and Ronnie up at Wintergreen. What time—six?'' She muttered something about the residents eating early, and he scribbled a note to himself. Not that he was likely to forget.

"Okay, five-thirty it is. And don't worry about food. Nettie's got a whole fridge full of stuff that

Dad and Mom will never eat. I just happen to know that today is her baking day.''

''You don't have to do that, Gar. It's not necessary. I can grab something from the deli.''

''Why bother? Now, get to work. You've got a lot of planning to do.'' He grinned, pleased that he'd been able to do this much for her.

''I do, don't I?'' Her voice thrilled with wonder.

Gar hung up, filled with determination to be there when Beth encountered Mervyn. If the old man was in one of his foul moods, he'd hightail Beth out of there so fast her head would spin. Potluck or no potluck.

He picked up the phone and called home. ''Hey, Nettie. This is your favorite person. No, not Ty.'' He grimaced, unwilling to accept that he'd been replaced in the cook's hierarchy of love. ''Gar. Your *very* favorite. What can you give me to take to the potluck at the nursing home tonight?''

As he listened to the string of items that ensued, Gar finally answered the voice inside his head. No, he didn't feel guilty. And he wasn't trying to buy Beth—not that he could. He simply wanted to help an old friend get past this next hurdle. If it meant spending some time with her, so much the better. He'd take whatever time he could get.

There wasn't anything wrong with seizing opportunity, was there?

# Chapter Five

"The whole town must be here." Ronnie almost danced up the sidewalk, her arms laden with the fresh rolls Nettie had donated for the potluck supper.

"And then some." Beth glanced around nervously, spying several vehicles she knew, and a lot of faces she recognized but couldn't put a name to. "I probably shouldn't have come. The Arnetts are having that big anniversary party on Saturday and I've got tons of work to do."

It was a stupid time for a reunion, she admitted privately. Why hadn't she come here one afternoon when Ronnie was in school and spoken to her father alone, without any witnesses?

*Because you were afraid he'd rant and rave like the last time. And you know he's right. You could have brought Ronnie to see him umpteen times in the past ten years.*

Yeah, I could have. But why would I?

*So she and Mervyn could get to know each other. Ronnie's not like you. She doesn't hold grudges.*

"Are you okay, Beth?" Gar's hand beneath her arm lent support that she was only too ready to accept.

"Yes, I'm fine. I just wish I hadn't come. There are so many people." She walked slowly through the doors and down the hall, barely following Ronnie's eager form as she burst her way through the crowd in a rush of energy.

"And they're all busy with their own families," Gar murmured in her ear. "No one is paying any attention to you."

It was a lie, but it was a nice lie.

"Yeah, they are," she muttered, nodding at the groups of people they passed. "And why not? The last time I was here, they had to sedate my father. Not exactly a great reunion." She heard a chortle and turned to look.

Gar's mouth was creased into a huge grin; his eyes danced with mirth. "Sorry. I just got this mental picture and—"

"It set you off." She shook her head in reproof, amazed that he hadn't lost his sense of the absurd. "Still, Gar?"

He shrugged. "I can't help it if I have a good sense of humor."

"More like a distorted one." She felt the tension draining away as his eyes laughed down into hers. She shrugged. "Okay, maybe it was kind of funny. In a weird sort of way."

"There you go." He stopped inside the huge dining room. "Is there someplace I can put this stuff, or am I doomed forever to carry three dozen butter tarts."

"Shh!" Beth placed a finger across his lips. "If you blab it to everyone, there will be none left." Suddenly she realized what she'd done and jerked her hand away.

Gar seemed unfazed. "There won't anyway," he prophesied, gloom distorting his handsome features. "Nettie's cooking never hangs around for very long." Then he grinned, and the blaze of it warmed her cold heart. "Fortunately, I have personal access to a private stash in the freezer. So, do you see him anywhere?"

"There. With Ronnie." Beth pointed to the small, shrunken man who sat huddled in an armchair, his eyes searching the room. When he saw her his eyes widened, but it was the sight of Gar that seemed to shake the old man.

Beth strode across the room, determined to get it over with. "Hi, Dad. How are you?"

The question was perfunctory, and everyone, including Mervyn, knew it.

"Cold," he barked, glaring at them. "Stupid place never cranks the heat up. Drafty old place." He jerked his chair forward, away from the window-ledge he'd sat down beside, and in so doing almost upset Gar's load of tarts. "What's that stuff?"

"Food." Gar set the containers down on a nearby coffee table and then shrugged out of his coat.

Beth couldn't help but notice the quality of the blue cashmere sweater he wore, and contrast it with her own acrylic pullover. There was no comparison. It was like comparing diamonds to cubic zirconias. She swallowed as he tugged the sweater off, displaying his powerful chest concealed by a black turtleneck.

"Put this on, Mr. Ainslow," he offered, holding out the expensive sweater. "I'm roasting. If I wear that I'll pass out for sure."

The room wasn't overly warm, but neither was it cold. Beth knew he was just being kind. But she couldn't afford to pay for that sweater. Neither could her father.

"Isn't it lovely, Dad?" Ronnie slid a hand over the knitted garment. "It's so soft. Here, I'll help you." She carefully slipped the oversize garment over the white head and then tenderly smoothed each hair back in place as her father shifted the sweater into place. "You look very nice."

"Feels better. Thank you." Mervyn studied Gar for so long that Beth wanted to scream. "Do I know you?"

"Garrett Winthrop. Charles's son. How are you, Mr. Ainslow?"

"Didn't think I knew you, but I expect you know right well how I am." Mervyn glared at the outstretched hand, but finally shook it. "When are we going to eat, anyway? A body could die of starvation in this place."

"I'm hungry, too. Should we find a table or something?" Ronnie glanced around, apparently unabashed by the grumpy behavior.

Beth could have crawled into a hole. Her own

father looked right past her as if she weren't even there. Why had she even bothered to come?

"I expect you're pretty proud of your daughters, aren't you, Mr. Ainslow? My brother tells me that Ronnie's in the running for a scholarship for her high marks. And Beth's shop is doing very well."

"Flowers!" The old man snorted. "Who needs that drivel in a dinky little town like Oakburn? It'll never fly."

"Actually it's flying higher than anyone expected." Gar's voice was even as he seated himself across from the older man, his gray eyes intent. "Beth's moving into a new building pretty soon, you know. She needs the extra space."

The sting of her father's words faded just a little as Beth listened to the proud ring in Gar's voice. He was such a wonderful man, spending his valuable time here, trying to coax a grumpy old man to smile.

"Humph! How's she going to pay for it?" Mervyn glanced at her for a minute, and Beth could see the malice in his eyes. "Your dad going to fund this expedition, too?"

"The bank has given her a loan." Gar's tones were even, though he cast an odd, questioning look at Beth.

"You got it?" Ronnie flew across the small area and hugged Beth. "Oh, how lovely! Now we can really show off your stuff. Wait 'til good old Oakburn sees those Valentine's arrangements you've got planned! The ones you did last year were awesome, but *these!* We'll have to hire someone to handle the extra customers."

"It is exciting, isn't it?" Beth turned back to her father, holding out the bouquet of flowers she carried. "I brought these over for your room. I thought they might cheer you up."

"How're flowers supposed to cheer me up?" Mervyn grumped, but there was a glint of something in his eye. "I suppose you'd better put them in my room, then. Ronnie, go put those things in a jar of water, would you?"

"Sure thing, Dad." Ronnie took the flowers and danced off down the hall, barely containing her excitement.

"Girl's full of vim and vinegar," Mervyn murmured appreciatively. "She'll go far in life."

"I hope so." Beth sank down into the nearest vacant chair and smoothed her slacks nervously. "She wants to go to veterinary school, you know."

"Smart girl! She can make a bundle off them rich folks that have their animals doctored all the time." Mervyn peered up at Gar quizzically. "Wasn't it a Winthrop who used to dole out a king's ransom for someone to take care of horses. Waste of money."

"Dad loves his horses. He doesn't consider that a waste." Gar smiled pleasantly at the curmudgeon, and then turned to Beth. "I think he recognizes me," he whispered. "He's just faking it."

"Why bother?" she asked back, and then sat up as an aide came to speak to them. "Yes, we'll be glad to sit over there. We brought these." She handed over the food and then grasped her father's elbow. "Come on, Dad. I'll help you up."

"I don't need help getting out of a chair!" Mervyn slapped her outstretched hand away before slowly standing.

Once erect, he wavered back and forth. Beth held her breath, afraid he'd fall down. She breathed a sigh of relief when Gar finally took her father's arm and led him toward the tables. Ronnie caught up with them halfway there.

"We'd better get seated pretty quick or we won't get a seat at all," he said, steering Mervyn toward a table near the window on the farside of the room. "This looks like a good spot."

"The cat comes in and out that door. I hate cats. Sneaky, preying things." Mervyn frowned. "It's cold here."

"You'll soon be warm. Now, Beth and I will go get some food while you and Ronnie save our places. What would you like?" Gar stood patiently waiting, seemingly unperturbed by the other man's continuous complaints.

"I suppose it's all cold stuff. What does a man have to do to get a hot meal around here?"

"I'll ask." Before Beth could say anything, Gar was escorting her toward the buffet. "Come on. I'll choose his plate. There must be something here that he likes."

"He used to love fried chicken. Not mine, of course. It wasn't as good as Mom's. Not that that ever stopped him from eating it!" She took four plates and handed him two. "I really appreciate your helping out, Gar. I'm just sorry he's so miserable today. It's not very pleasant for you, and you've been so kind."

"Beth, don't worry about me. I'm fine. I just feel kind of sorry for your dad. He's stuck there all day, staring out the window, when you know he'd rather be snowshoeing across country. He used to love to hunt, didn't he?"

Beth was surprised. "I didn't know you'd remember that. It was a long time ago." She thought about her father's change of life-style. "I guess it is sort of constricting. But I can't look after him properly at Wintergreen. He needs oxygen most of the time, and medication for his heart. I'd have to stay home." She shook her head in frustration. "It's a no-win situation."

Gar's hand covered hers. "You're doing the best you can, Beth. Nobody could ask for more than that. Besides, I'm not so sure your father would want to live with you. He seems to have made a few friends here."

He tilted his head to one side, and Beth followed the motion, then gasped as her father's hearty laugh rang out, his face wreathed in a grin as he joked with an elderly woman who shuffled past in her walker.

"He's smiling," she breathed in astonishment. "Imagine!"

"Yeah, imagine." But Gar was staring at her, his face intent. "Don't start to feel guilty, Beth. You did the best you could. That's the most you could do."

She put a scoop of potato salad on Ronnie's plate, then served herself with lettuce.

"He blames me, you know," she said finally,

aware that though he kept moving through the line, Gar was waiting for her next response. "He said I should have at least brought Ronnie to see him, even if she didn't stay with him. He doesn't seem to understand that I wasn't just a few miles away. I couldn't simply pack her up and send her, and it would have cost so much for both of us to fly down."

Gar picked up a couple of rolls and butter, waited for Beth to add meat to her plates, and then stepped aside, out of the way of scurrying staff.

"Did you want to?" he asked softly.

Beth searched his face, but there was nothing there to hint at malice. He wasn't just chipping away at her. He really wanted to know. Slowly, she shook her head.

"No, I didn't. I never wanted to come back here, even if we could have afforded it. When I left this place back then, I thought I'd left for good."

He nodded. "You did the best you could. Let it go."

As she followed him back to the table and watched her father scrutinize the choices Gar had made for him, Beth couldn't help wondering how she was supposed to let the past go when her father wouldn't.

Two hours later they left the home, Ronnie running back to tell her father one last thing she'd forgotten to impart.

"Those two seem to really hit it off." Gar grinned. "Not that your sister has a problem talking to anyone, but she seems really close to your dad."

Beth nodded. "It's one of the reasons I came back, even though he seems to hate me. Ronnie really needed this connection to her family. I just hope I won't live to regret it."

"What do you mean?" Gar stood, frowning, as he held the car door open. "Why should you regret it?"

"You don't know what he's like when he takes a drink, Gar. If he ever gets hold of a bottle, he'll stomp all over her tender feelings. Alcohol doesn't bring out the best in him."

Gar slammed the door shut and walked around to the other side. He climbed in and started the car, switching the heater on high before he spoke.

"There is no liquor allowed where he's staying, Beth. And anyway, I'm sure he's past that now. You yourself said it was partly because of your mother's death. That was a long time ago. He's had time to deal with it."

Beth pulled her wallet out of her purse and opened it to display the photo she'd tucked inside so long ago. "This was my mom, Gar," she murmured, holding it out so he could get a better look.

"You could be identical twins!" Gar stared at her, then at the photo. "It's amazing."

"Maybe now you see why he finds it so hard to have me around, why he resents me. I must remind him of her constantly."

"Yes, I suppose you must." Gar stared at the photo until Ronnie returned to the car, breathless and chatty.

"He's playing cribbage with some other old guy.

They have quite a sparring match going, but I don't think Dad will better him.'' Ronnie perched on the edge of the back seat so she could pat Gar's shoulder. ''Thanks for backing Beth up. He razzes her a lot, and I know it hurts her.''

''Maybe you can drop me at the store,'' Beth broke in, her face warm with embarrassment. ''I have a fair bit of work to do there. Will you be okay for a while, Ronnie?''

''Aw, come on, sis! You promised I could have Ty over tonight. We're working on that biology project together, and I was going to help him decide on the title page.''

''He's doing the title page and—let me guess—'' Gar pretended to consider for a moment ''—you're doing all the work, right? That kid is a freeloader.''

''No, he's not!'' Ronnie protested indignantly, her eyes flashing. ''Ty's been a really great friend. Besides, I'm just repaying him.''

''Repaying him? For what?'' Beth frowned, wondering how she was ever to keep up to the orders that had begun to flood in if she was constantly chaperoning teenagers.

''Just a little agreement the two of us had. Nothing bad, really. He's helping me with a little problem, and I'm helping him.'' Ronnie leaned back in her seat. ''It's okay if you can't handle it tonight, sis. I know you've got to get those orders ready. I guess I'll have to phone Ty as soon as we get home. I hope he hasn't left yet.'' That plaintive note crept into her voice.

''I could stay.'' Gar's response was hesitant, almost apologetic. "I haven't got anything scheduled for tonight but paperwork, and even that isn't urgent. I don't mind watching the two of them at Wintergreen. Or they can come out to Fairwinds. Mom and Dad would like that."

"That's very kind of you—" Beth stared at her sister's vehemently shaking head.

"No, we can't do that. It has to be at Wintergreen. I've got all my research and stuff already set up there in the library we made. It'll take me eons to pack it all up and then unpack it. Besides—" Ronnie checked her watch "—Ty should be showing up right about now."

Gar turned the corner, and, sure enough, there was Ty climbing out of his father's luxurious sedan, which then pulled away.

Ronnie burst out of Gar's car and sprinted over to where Ty stood. A hurriedly whispered conversation took place. Beth sighed and accepted the hand Gar offered as she levered herself out of the low-slung sports car. Whatever they were up to, it was apparently top secret. But she wouldn't pry. Let Ronnie have her secrets. At least something besides her father was occupying the girl's mind.

"Ty and I would really like to have Gar stay. If it's okay with you, Beth?" Ronnie's wistful expression was the same one she used to wheedle extra candy out of her sister every Christmas.

Beth had never been able to resist Ronnie's soft doe-eyed look, so she turned to Gar. "What do you think?"

"I think she should find somebody else to con,"

he muttered for her ears alone. "I also think that you're too soft. If you don't want me here, just say so."

"Oh, no. It's not that. It's just that I was worried that you'd have something else to do. Something more important." Beth knew she was babbling. She clamped her lips together while she searched for her misplaced decorum. "If you don't mind hanging around here, it's fine with me. I just don't think it's a good idea for them to be alone here."

"I agree." He followed her up the stairs and into the house. "With those two in cahoots, Wintergreen would probably be reduced to hundred-year-old ashes in mere minutes." He patted a balustrade fondly. "Since I like what Caitlin's done with the old girl, I'll protect her."

"Oh, brother!" Beth rolled her eyes as she unlocked her door. "Here you are, then. Enjoy, soak up the ambience, or whatever it is. I'm going back to the shop."

"I could take you," Gar offered. "These two could manage for five minutes."

Beth shook her head, smiling as she thrust her keys back in her pocket. "No, thanks. Climbing out of that thing more than twice a day is dangerous to my health."

"You don't like my Vette all of a sudden?" His eyebrows rose. "Why?"

Beth pulled on her gloves, relishing her response even before she gave it. Gar was pleased with himself, a little too pleased that she'd been coerced into doing what Ronnie wanted. His shoulders were all puffed up with conceit and his eyes glittered the way they always had when he thought he'd snuck in the last word.

"Garrett Winthrop, you aren't sixteen years old anymore. That's a hot rod, a toy car. It's not the kind of vehicle a man who advises people on their finances should drive. It's too—" She searched for the right word. "Risky," she finally managed.

"Risky?" He looked affronted. "My car isn't risky! It's got a powerful motor that can overtake most anything on the roads around here."

Beth nodded, biting her lip to keep from smiling. "I know. And when people look at you sitting in that shiny black bat-car, what do you think they see?"

"I dunno." Confusion crossed his face. "What do you see?"

"A little boy who never grew up." She pulled open the door, then turned back and wiggled her fingers at him. "See you later."

"Beth, wait a minute! What do you mean? I'm not a kid—"

She shut the door on his protestations and burst out laughing. *That* would give him something to think about aside from her shabby furniture and cheap furnishings.

Now, if she could just keep her mind off him for the next couple of hours, she might actually get some work done.

# Chapter Six

"Folks, if we can bring this meeting to order." Herbert Fitzwater pounded the hammer, which was acting as a gavel, on the block of spruce. "Come on, folks. We've got us some business to do here tonight."

Gar glanced around the table, searching for but not finding Beth's tiny figure. Where was she? He'd volunteered for this committee, and Beth was the only reason he was here. He had figured he could almost call it a date, and it was sure better than sitting for three hours in her living room, staring at blissful, smiling photos of her, Denis and Ronnie as he had during his last visit to Wintergreen.

So where was she?

"All right now. That's better." Herbert grinned his semi-toothless smile, and pawed through the sheaf of papers in front of him. "Now, what's next, Eustace?"

"You might call the roll, Herbert. How d'we know if everybody's here? We can't just hope we got all our members."

Gar knew Edgar Bonds wasn't in the least happy with being included on this board. What he did like was the stipend he was paid for attending. This was probably his one contribution of the night, but Gar could have kissed him for it. Surely now they wouldn't start without Beth.

"I counted seven around this table, Ed. That's the number we're s'posed to have. Now let's get down to business."

Gar was about to protest, ask for a recount, do something—anything—to stop them, when the door to the council chambers flew open and Beth rushed inside. Her cheeks were red from the cold and her hair stood up in little golden-red spikes that the wind had created.

"I'm so sorry. I had a last-minute customer." She tugged her coat off as she spoke and placed it across one of the empty tables.

Since no one else moved, Gar got up and offered her his chair. Once she was seated, he retrieved another for himself and set it to the left of hers, raising one eyebrow at Gertrude McGillicuddy in the hope that she would move her chair just a tad south.

"Excuse me," he whispered as Herbert slammed the hammer down once more. Gertrude frowned ferociously, but did eventually shift her considerable bulk enough to let him find a place at the table. Beth pushed his writing tablet and folder over, and he took them with a smile.

"Put that hammer away before you hurt someone, Herbert!" Gertrude sniffed and leaned her shoulders back against the chair, her chin jutting out in anger. "Let's get on with it, shall we? And we're supposed to be eight, not seven, if you check the latest roster that clerk printed. You never could count."

Somewhat abashed by the crankiness of his former schoolteacher, Herbert laid down his hammer and began explaining exactly what their duties were to be. "Now, we've already got the building. Tom Pettigrew set that up for us by organizing the old town hall. What we have to do now is decide what's to go in the place and how it's to be run. Anybody got any suggestions?"

"I do." Beth's voice jerked Gar out of his in-depth study of her fingernails. "I think it's imperative that the center, once it's set up, not depend on the town for huge amounts of money. I've taken the liberty of drawing up a proposal for a budget, using the amount that the town has already allocated to furnish the center."

Gar accepted his copy in stunned disbelief. Surely this was his field. Shouldn't he have been approached to run the financial aspects of the whole thing? Not that it mattered. Beth probably hadn't considered the depreciation of the building or the need for a canteen or something like it. And there would have to be revenues to offset some of the expense. He glanced down and swallowed his smug feeling of superiority as he read over her proposal.

"Garrett, you're the head honcho when it comes to new business in Oakburn. What do you think of this?'' Edgar, newly roused from his sleep by Gertrude's wayward cane, waved his papers back and forth across the table, creating a slight draft that sent the others scattering to rescue their fluttering pages. ''Does she know what she's talking about?''

Yipes! Now they'd done it. Beth would be furious. And he didn't blame her. Who wanted to be put down by an oaf like Edgar? He stared at the sheets she'd handed out, searching for an answer as he got to his feet.

*What do I say, Lord? I don't want to hurt her feelings.*

Tell the truth.

Ha! That was easier said than done. Gar kept his head bent, kept his eyes on the paper.

''Garrett?'' Herbert thunked the table again. ''Has the boy gone deaf? Poke him, Gertie.''

Gertrude straightened, her face a tight mask. Garrett knew they were about to witness an all-out war between two angry factions that had been feuding for as long as he could remember. He had to do something. When in doubt, stall.

''Just a minute, Herbert. I'm reading.'' Gar forced his eyes back on the page and prayed desperately for a way out of this debacle. He didn't want to be involved in another of these petty disputes that the senior citizens waged just for the fun of keeping their wits sharp.

*Come on, Lord. What am I supposed to say now?*

''Speak the truth in love.''

''Well?'' Edgar had awakened long enough to glare at them all balefully.

"I think," Gar began, feeling his way as he went, "that we should ask Beth, er, Miss Ainslow, to explain these to us. She's gone to a lot of work on this." He smiled at Beth, then sank down onto his chair with relief. Whew, that was close.

"He's right. I have spent a good deal of time researching the number of young people likely to use the center in the next five years because I want to make sure that it's a place where my sister, among others, can enjoy herself without getting into trouble."

Gar listened in amazement as Beth calmly and clearly delineated her study for everyone's benefit. He couldn't fault her on either presentation or accuracy. She'd researched her subject well, and had obviously come prepared to deal with any skepticism she found.

"Any questions?"

He felt so proud of her, standing there, her hair glowing in the bright fluorescent light.

"Very thorough. Always did think a woman was better at these things." Gertrude crossed her arms over her thin chest with smug satisfaction as she glowered up the table at Herbert. "I say, let's go ahead with it."

"Not so fast, Gertie. I want to know where she got all this information. And how are we going to pay for all this stuff she says these kids need?" Eustace tented his fingers and peered at them as if he'd never seen such beauty before. "In my day we made do with a sled and a hill. Or we talked and listened to the radio. We didn't need Ping-Pong tables and CD players.'' He snorted in disgust.

Gar sat where he was, marveling that Eustace had managed to say so much at one time. He jerked to life when a sharp finger jabbed him in the ribs. Gertrude was scowling.

"Pay attention, boy!"

"I studied several different youth facilities in towns across the state. The successful ones had certain planned events, but a lot of the time the centers operate like an open house between set hours. Of course an adult or two is always in-house, just in case, but mostly the kids are responsible for the property themselves.''

"How do they manage that?" Edgar sniffed derisively. "I can't even get my kids to look after their bikes."

"Not firm enough." Gertrude nodded knowingly, her face pinched and tight. "That's the problem with parents today. They want to blame everything on their children, when they're simply too weak to make rules and abide by them."

"My kids are no worse…" As Edgar launched into a spiel about the youth of today, Gar got to his feet.

"Excuse me," he said loudly. "Point of order, Mr. Chairman."

"What?" Herbert jerked to attention, knocking the hammer to the floor; it narrowly missed his toes. "What is it?"

"If we are to make any progress tonight, I think we need to get on with business. Now, Miss Ainslow has given us plenty to think about. Economically, I'm sure you'll all agree that her plan is very workable. What we should focus on is finding some funding for this project."

"I was kind of enjoying hearing about Ed's brats, but I suppose you're right." Herbert conceded the point with regret. "What do you suggest, Miss Ainslow?"

"Please, I've been Beth for twenty-eight years now. I think you can still call me that." Beth grinned, then shrugged. "Actually, I think the kids themselves should be invited to attend our meeting. There's no point in planning something they don't want. If they're in at the beginning, they can suggest fund-raising ideas that they'll be willing to help in."

"Let the kids be part of it?" Herbert considered this soberly.

Gertrude McGillicuddy wasn't quite so hesitant. She turned to Gar and frowned. "The girl has a good solid brain," she murmured, just loud enough for the whole room to hear. "Seems to me you messed up good when you let her go."

Gar heard Beth gasp. He knew that she would insist on setting the record straight, but, for once, he didn't want that. "Yes, I sure did, Miss McGillicuddy. I messed up very badly."

Gertrude pinned him with the same look that had cowed every kid in her Sunday school class. "Time to learn from your mistakes, isn't it?"

Gar nodded, glancing toward Beth. "Way past time," he murmured.

"Maybe you're right, Gar. We should study

this." Never one to make a decision hastily, Herbert gathered together his papers and nodded sagely. "Okay, so we'll meet next week, same time, and let the kids have their say. Meeting adjourned." The hammer retrieved, Herbert slammed it against the board, which promptly split in two.

"Well, that was quick." Gar got to his feet, a grin itching at the corners of his mouth as he watched the others speedily vacate the room. "You sure know how to clear a room."

Beth made a face. "I'm not so sure I can take all the credit." She chuckled. "They didn't look any too pleased to be here when I came in. Besides, I'm pretty sure there's an important hockey game at the rink tonight."

"Want to go for coffee and discuss the next step? I'm sure you've got it planned out. You seem to have done a lot of work on this project. I don't know how you find the time." He placed her prospectus carefully inside his folder and shoved the folder in his briefcase. "There's a ton of information here. I didn't realize you had so much experience at this. Glynis said your loan application was more complete than any she's seen in a long time."

"Thank you. But you don't have to say that."

He saw the blush color her cheeks a faint pink, and guessed she'd had few compliments on her business acumen.

"I never say anything I don't mean." He held out her coat. "Coffee?"

She studied him with a wary look. "I guess. The kids are at my place studying again. At least, that's what they're supposed to be doing. Caitlin's going to check on them." She slid her arms into the sleeves, and murmured a thank-you when he set the heavy wool on her shoulders.

"They seem to be whispering a lot these days. Whenever I come into the room it stops, and Ty gets this sad, innocent look on his face. He used it when he stayed for supper tonight, too. What do you suppose they're up to?"

Gar slid on his own jacket and shrugged. "I have no clue. And, to tell you the truth, I don't want to know. It's too scary." He grinned to show he was joking. "Though I will tell you that lately I've begun to realize that shielding Ty from Dad's anger isn't always the best thing. It's better for him to face up to his responsibilities."

"What responsibilities?" Beth asked as she bundled her information back into the leather portfolio she carried. One last glance at the long polished table and she led the way to the door. "He's barely eighteen. Besides helping out with the horses, which he adores, what else is there for him to be responsible for around Fairwinds? Your parents have a huge staff to take care of things."

Gar nodded, holding the outside door of the municipal offices open for her.

"Yes, I know. But there are certain things Dad expects from his sons. Up to now, Ty has avoided hearing too much about that. Mostly because I've shielded him."

"And now?" Beth hugged her case close. "What's changed?"

"For one thing, he's getting older. He won't be in school forever. Ty's going to have to decide on his future. Dad would like to have him in the bank, of course." He held out his arm. "You'd better take my arm. In those heels you'll land flat on your, er, back." He grinned at her frown, then grabbed her arm when she tripped on a ripple of ice. "See?"

"I don't know what it is about my shoes that makes people feel they have to comment on them. I like heels. They make me feel like someone somewhere might actually notice what I have to say. It's no fun being a shrimp, you know." Her fingers deliberately pinched a little tighter as she slipped and slid her way over to his car.

"I have nothing against your choice of footwear, Beth, so you needn't frown like that. I was merely offering an opinion about the likelihood of your remaining upright while prancing about on the ice in those." He raised one eyebrow as she swung her legs into the car. "Although, I suppose you could dig your heels in like spikes."

He burst out laughing at her indignant look, but managed to hide the fact as he slammed the door shut and walked around the car. By the time he was inside, next to her, he'd organized his face into a mask of control.

"Now, what were we talking about?" he asked innocently after shifting into gear.

"Ty," she returned immediately. Her forehead pleated in a frown as she peered up at him through the gloom. "What if he doesn't want to go into banking, Gar? What if he wants something completely different for himself?''

Gar stared at her, his brain working. Something his brother had said earlier pricked at his brain, but for the life of him he couldn't remember exactly what. He shoved the thought away. It didn't matter. What bugged him now was why she was asking.

''Not go into banking?'' Gar laughed. ''Why wouldn't he? Ty isn't the most industrious person in the world, and the bank is already set up. He can slide into place with a minimum of fuss. It's perfect for him.''

''Is it?'' Beth looked as if she wanted to say more but didn't dare.

Several minutes elapsed as he drove to the coffee house on the edge of town.

''Did you always want to work with your dad?'' Beth pressed. ''Didn't you ever dream of starting something yourself? Something that was totally yours, with *your* name on it?''

''The bank has my name on it. At least, it's where it counts—on the bottom line.'' Gar risked a glance at her face and found her peering out the window at the passing businesses. ''I've always known I was being groomed to take Dad's place, just as he took his father's place. What's wrong with that?''

''Oh, there's nothing wrong with it. As long as that's what you want to do. I was just wondering what would happen if you had decided you wanted to study, say, geology. Maybe be an astronaut. Or maybe find a cure for cancer.'' She spared him a glance, then resumed her scrutiny of the empty town streets.

"A doctor? Me?" He laughed. "I don't think so. Numbers have always been my preference, Beth. You know that. Surely you can't have forgotten our math tutoring sessions?" He winked at her, hoping she'd remember how little time they'd actually spent on the problems cited in the texts.

But Beth only smiled vacantly, her big green eyes clouded with something he couldn't name.

"I remember," she murmured. "I remember everything."

Gar was so busy studying her, he almost missed the vehicle that careened through the intersection. The big shiny cab of a semi narrowly missed his bumper as it sped through a red light. He jammed on his brakes and yanked the steering wheel hard right, hoping to avoid any further damage from the truck's cargo, which followed obediently behind the cab.

In slow motion he saw the tractor-trailer slide past them, its big, unwieldly length ready to cut off their avenue of escape. He hit the brakes hard, praying for help as he tried to steer a separate path.

The icy patches negated any braking prowess he had, and Gar played with the wheel as they slid uncontrollably. Everything moved so fast that he could only hold his breath and pray Beth would escape. Seconds later, through some miracle of rubber on ice, they were heading toward the curb as the semi roared past, horn honking. The car came to a grinding halt mere inches from the yellow cement curb.

"Are you okay?" He turned his head and found Beth jammed against his side, her face white as a sheet as she hung on to his arm. Her seat belt held her in place, but it didn't stop the fear from crowding into her eyes. He took her arm. "Beth, are you okay?"

She nodded slowly, her fingers tightening on the fabric of his jacket. "I thought we were going to slide right under it," she gasped. "We could have been killed!"

"We're fine. It's okay." Gar gathered her shaking body into his arms and held her for several moments, willing the fear to recede. "Nothing happened. You're all right. I've got you."

When she finally stopped shivering, he leaned back to peer down into her face. What he saw there made his breath catch.

"Beth?"

She stared at him the way he remembered from so long ago, and to Gar, time retreated back to those glorious days when he'd been totally and completely in love. The longing he saw reflected in her eyes echoed that of his own heart, and he couldn't stop himself from brushing the red-gold strands off her forehead and tracing his lips across the thin, delicate alabaster skin.

"Oh, Beth. I've missed you so much." When she didn't answer, just clung a little tighter to his lapels, Gar bent his head and took her lips, tasting their sweetness like a man denied sustenance.

And wonder of wonders, Beth returned his embrace. Her hands pulled him closer, her lips met his and answered their request with one of her own.

When she finally pulled away, Gar was lost in a world of make-believe, where he and Beth were walking down the aisle together.

"I'm sorry. I shouldn't have done that." She straightened back into her own seat, her face warm with the blush that made her freckles stand out on her pert nose.

Gar lifted a hand to trace them, and then remembered that this wasn't the past. This was the here and now.

"I don't want your apology," he mumbled, shifting in his own seat. He tilted his chin defiantly and dared her to look away from him. "I enjoyed kissing you. I always have. You probably forgot."

"I haven't forgotten anything."

He barely heard her response, so soft was her voice. Perhaps she hadn't meant for him to hear. But though he searched her face for an answer, she shut him out. The pixie face that could flash in a grin of amusement or freeze in a mask of disdain was now frustratingly empty, devoid of all response.

"Perhaps you'd better take me home," she murmured. "I don't really feel much like coffee anymore. Besides, the kids will wonder what happened."

"I doubt that," he muttered. But he did as she asked, making an illegal U-turn in the middle of the now-deserted street. "Should *I* apologize?"

"No, of course not. Put it down to the moment," she scoffed. But she avoided his eyes.

"It wasn't the moment," he told her honestly, enjoying her frustrated glance. "I've been wanting to kiss you for ages." She was going to interrupt, so Gar switched tactics. "Beth, my grandmother has been asking me to bring you for a visit. I wondered if you'd come Sunday after church."

"Your grandmother?" She stopped, thought for a moment, then raised her eyebrows. "But doesn't she live in Paris or something?"

"She did, until my grandfather died five years ago. Then she only wanted to come home. Now she lives just outside of town on a small acreage in the hills, near my place. I usually stop in at least once a day."

"I didn't know you had a place, either." She grimaced. "I guess I'm still a little behind the times."

"I built it when I moved back here. When I still believed you were coming back." He watched for some flicker of surprise, but sometime in the past few years Beth had become more adept at hiding her emotions. Only a spark of interest flickered in her eyes.

"Why would your grandmother want to meet me? We have nothing in common."

She avoided his admission so easily. She was running scared, ignoring everything to do with the past. Gar smiled a half smile. It was a good start. At least she wasn't indifferent to him. He'd take what he could get and run with it.

"Well? Is Sunday suitable? Shall I tell her you'll come?" He pressed home his request, anxious to ensure that his two favorite women finally met.

"I think Ronnie wants to go to see Dad on Sunday."

"We'll drop her off on our way. After we've had lunch." He had it all planned out. Now, if he could just get her to cooperate.

"You don't have to buy us lunch. I always put something on to cook while we're at the service. Why don't you come to our place?"

It was on the tip of his tongue to refuse, to insist that she deserved a break, a trip to the nicest place in town. But something in her eyes stopped him.

"Okay, that'd be great. Can I bring something?"

She laughed, and it was a light tinkling sound that made the world seem a better place. Gar couldn't tamp down the hope that sprang up inside.

"What's so funny?"

"You are! Exactly what would you like to bring? What's your specialty, Gar? If I remember correctly, you set the kitchen at Fairwinds on fire once. Have things changed so much?" She giggled at his affronted look. "I didn't think so."

"I can cook. A few things." He pulled up in front of Wintergreen and parked the car before turning to face her. "I can. I make a good pot of tea. And I know how to make toast and those pizza things you put in the microwave."

"You *have* come a long way!" Beth's voice mocked his accomplishments. "For a guy who used to routinely incinerate everything he touched, I guess that's progress." She opened her door and climbed out, then leaned in to add, "Don't bother bringing anything, Gar. Except maybe Ty, so Ronnie will have somebody to talk to.''

Gar climbed out of the car and walked around it, then took her arm before marching her up the shoveled walk to the house.

''Seems like we've always got those two around,'' he muttered, rolling his eyes as two heads peeked out from behind Beth's door. ''See what I mean?''

Beth stamped the snow off her boots and led the way inside. ''They're harmless,'' she chided. ''Take your coat off. I'll make some coffee. And you can sample Ronnie's cookies.''

She turned away quickly, so Gar did as she said, convinced by her manner that there was something she wasn't telling him. Or maybe it was just the aftereffects of their near-accident?

''Hi, you two. Get any studying done?'' He frowned as Ty made some secret hand signal to Ronnie. ''I guess not.''

''We got a lot done, actually, Gar. Ronnie's really good at biology, even if I'm a dud.''

''You're not a dud. You just don't care about it like I do. Besides, you got a way higher mark in home economics than I did.'' Ronnie's eyes sparkled with teasing as she glanced from Gar to her sister and then back again.

''You're taking home economics?'' Gar wondered what else he'd missed. ''Why?''

''No choice. The school has this brilliant idea that the males of the species are not properly prepared to fend for themselves when they get out into the big, wide world. Guess they think we're all as incompetent as you, bro.''

Beth stuck her head out of the tiny kitchen. "He's not incompetent, Ty. He just *really likes* all those forms of carbon."

When they all burst out laughing at him, Gar decided it was time to turn the tables. "It's not as if you take after your sister, Ronnie. She never did catch onto biology, either, even after Mrs. Beetle diagrammed the inside of a cow's stomach."

"Yech!" Ty pretended to gag. "More than I needed to know."

"I guess everybody has a talent. My home ec teacher says I shouldn't plan on owning a restaurant." She sighed. "I can't understand why Mrs. Arnold gets so worked up when I alter her recipes. It's not as if her heavy old bran muffins don't taste better with a few chocolate chips."

Ronnie disappeared into the kitchen and returned with a plate of charred, barely recognizable cookies, which she offered to Gar. "Try one of these. I substituted a few things, but they're not bad."

Gar reached out gingerly and lifted up the top one, which also happened to be the biggest. He bit into it experimentally, and then stopped as his teeth came into contact with something hard and unchewable.

"Aren't they good?" Behind Ronnie, Ty was making faces, holding his throat and openly mocking his brother.

"Different," Gar said. "I've never really tasted

anything like this before.'' He stopped when Beth appeared with a tray of hot chocolate.

''And you probably won't again, right?'' she muttered sotto voce. ''Can't say I blame you. Don't eat it all, or you'll get awful heartburn.''

''I substituted coconut for the peanut butter, and some cheese and stuff for the oil. I don't like greasy stuff.'' Ronnie seemed unperturbed by the color of the ghastly tasting concoction, never mind the charred edges and crisp chocolate chips. ''But I didn't change the chocolate. You should never alter chocolate.''

''Absolutely.'' Gar slipped the rest of his cookie into his pocket and gulped down a mouthful of the steaming hot chocolate. He glanced up in time to see Beth's wink. ''Come on, Ty. You need to get home. Your curfew isn't far off, and from what I've heard, you've missed a couple lately.''

''Aw, Gar!'' Tyler unfolded himself from the rug in front of the fireplace with a moan meant to sway the hardest heart.

''Forget it. I'm not covering for you in this, buddy. You're late, you take the heat. Let's go. Thanks for the hot chocolate, Beth. And the cookie, Ronnie.'' He took his coat from Beth and slid it on, checking to be sure her natural color had returned. ''By the way, Beth and I are going to Gran's on Sunday, Ty. Maybe you and Ronnie can think of something to do.''

Gar frowned as he watched his brother make the motions of a high-five behind Beth's back. ''What are you two planning now?'' he demanded.

"Us? Planning something?" Tyler gave a fake laugh that didn't quite come off. "Don't be silly, Garrett. What on earth would we be planning?"

"Yeah, like what? You make us sound like criminals. Come on, Tyler. I'll walk you out." Ronnie threaded her arm through Ty's.

"Walk me out? I can walk myself out. It's not like there's more than one door, Ron." Ty squawked once when the girl yanked on his arm. Then enlightenment seemed to dawn. "Oh, sure. Lead on, Macduff. Walk me out."

"They're acting very unusual, even for them. And they look guilty." Beth stood behind him, frowning at the retreating pair, who were whispering madly. They stopped once to glance back over their shoulders, then scurried out the door.

"I know it. I'm sure they're up to something. I just don't know what. Doesn't really matter, I suppose." He shrugged the feeling away and studied her once more. "You're okay? You won't have a bad dream or something?"

Beth grinned that spunky smirk that told him she probably would, but that she wouldn't admit anything of the sort to him. "I'm perfectly fine, Gar."

"That's good." He smiled, enjoying the curious look that came over her face when his arms slid around her waist.

"It is?" She stood peering up at him. "Why?"

"Because I'm going to kiss you good-night, and I don't want you blaming the effect on our traffic incident earlier."

"Oh."

She didn't move away, so Gar took that as a good sign.

"'Oh.' That's all you're going to say?" He frowned.

"What did you expect me to say?" Her jade eyes glinted.

"I don't know. Scream 'yes' maybe. Throw your arms around me and kiss me back. Act surprised. Something."

"Sorry." But she didn't move away, didn't lower the slim arms that had crept up to his shoulders.

Gar decided to quit wasting time. He held her face between his palms, bent his head and touched her mouth gently with his own, deepening the kiss when she responded.

"Gar, we have to— Oh, sorry." Ty left again in a hurried scramble, and then they were alone again.

"They're going to get the wrong idea," Beth whispered as she lowered her arms, her face touched with pink.

"What's the right idea?" he murmured, enjoying her confusion.

"No more questions. Good night, Garrett." Her laughter bubbled out, a joyful sound in the silent room.

"Good night." Knowing a good exit line when he heard one, Garrett grabbed this one and ran with it. "See you Sunday, if not before."

"Uh-huh."

He hastened out of the building and down to the end of the walk, turning just once to see her framed in a window, her arm flung across Ronnie's shoulders. Satisfied that she seemed back to normal, he climbed into the car and turned the volume knob of his CD player down to a dull roar.

"You two are getting pretty cozy. Especially when you're supposed to hate her guts." Tyler didn't bother pretending he hadn't seen anything. "I didn't notice Beth protesting, either."

Gar started the car and drove away from Wintergreen at a sedate fifteen miles an hour. "I don't hate her," he murmured. And the words rang true through his mind. "I never did."

"Sure sounded like hate to me the few times I heard you mention her name."

Not hate, Gar told himself with new awareness. I love her. More than I ever have. I love Beth Ainslow, and I couldn't care less if she had married six men. If she loves me, and I think she does, that's what I want more than anything.

"Did you hear me?" Ty asked, switching the stereo off. "I asked you a question. Should I repeat it?"

"No, Ty. And don't hold your breath waiting for an answer, because I'm not going to give you one."

"Why not?" Tyler's belligerent voice rang loudly through the car's small interior. "I want to know if you're going to date her again."

"That's none of your business, brother dear."

"Sure it is. I like her sister a lot. If you two are going to be fighting all the time, I'd like to know ahead of time. That way Ronnie and I can avoid both of you."

"We're not going to be fighting," Gar informed him, a tiny smile twitching at the edge of his mouth.

Now why was he so positive of that?

# Chapter Seven

"Are you willingly going to tell us about that meeting the night before last, or are we going to have to pry it out of you?" Caitlin looked determined enough to try, so Beth nodded.

"All right, I'll tell you both. But please don't read too much into it. Promise?"

"Oh, will you just spill it?" Maryann tossed her needlepoint onto a nearby chair, slipped her shoes off and crossed her feet beneath her. "And hurry up. You've kept us on tenterhooks for days."

"Hardly days. It was on Monday night."

"And this is Friday. Days." Maryann sniffed, nose in the air.

"Okay, days. I have been working this week, you know. Stop nagging me, Mare. Give me a break."

"I'm not nagging. It's perfectly reasonable to expect some details. You guys pried into my life— remember?"

"I've never pried!"

A shrill whistle barely stopped Maryann's exasperated protests. Beth whirled around to stare at Caitlin.

"You two are in my home, at my invitation, so I'll give the orders. Is that clear?" Caitlin stood, hands on her hips, as she regarded the other two with a glint in her eye.

"It's clear." Maryann sighed. "Sorry, Beth. I was nagging. Guess I'm just overly curious."

"So am I." Caitlin flopped down beside Beth and pointed a finger directly at her. "Now I'm ordering. You. Tell all. Now. Got it?"

"She's a tyrant. I wonder if Jordan knows." Beth held up both hands. "All right. I'm telling, I'm telling. We talked. That's all."

"And I'm the tooth fairy." Maryann nodded at Caitlin. "I heard they were seen parked on Main Street."

"You're kidding. Ooh." Caitlin fluttered her lashes and gave a coquettish laugh. "Just like the teenyboppers."

"We were parked there because we narrowly missed being killed." Beth nodded, smugly confident that she now had their full attention. "It's true. A semi went through on a red light, and we were in the intersection. It was scary."

"I'm sure it was, dear. But actually, I was enquiring about your meeting about the youth center. You remember the one. Garrett Winthrop also sits on that committee." Maryann smiled sweetly, her teeth bared in a threat.

"It was great. I could hardly believe it myself. Of course some of it was due to Gar." Beth fed them every detail she could remember, from presenting her proposal to Gar's asking the other committee members to give it a chance.

"So you see, Beth. You worried for nothing. Gar doesn't hate you. He obviously thinks you've got talent and brains if he got the others to read your paper." Caitlin nodded as if she'd known it all along.

"It felt so good to stand there and actually know what I was talking about. After the first few minutes, I felt like I could field any of their questions." Beth allowed herself to preen, just a bit. "I did the work, I organized it into a presentation, and last night we had a quick meeting with some of the youth. They're going to help out with a number of the decisions."

"Which is exactly what you wanted. Congratulations, girlfriend." Maryann thrust her hands into the air in a silent cheer. "I knew you could do it. You always were smart when you put your mind to it."

"No, Mare, I wasn't. That's the thing, you see. I've always felt so intimidated by people in power. I felt dumb and out of it." She shrugged, her lips lifting in a smile of remembrance. "But when I saw Miss McGillicuddy sniping at the others, I realized that they're just ordinary people like anyone else. And when it came to the center, I had more information than they did because I'd studied up on it. Gar even complimented me on my work."

"I don't know why not. You're smart as a whip, Beth. We've always known that. It's just taken *you* a while to figure it out." Caitlin smiled benignly.

Beth felt as if a sudden calm had collapsed her sails. "But don't you see? I'm finally on a par with the rest of the town. I can hold my own when it comes to a discussion. Gar and I were throwing around projected costs last night, and when he started doing a spreadsheet on his laptop, I knew exactly what he was talking about. It was great."

"Of course you knew that stuff, Bethy. You've got a degree in business, haven't you?" Maryann pretended to stifle the yawn that stretched her mouth wide.

"Well, yes. But still, it was quite something to feel as if I mattered."

"You're worrying me now, Beth Ainslow. You always mattered. And it doesn't mean a heap of nails to me that Gar or anybody else noticed it. God made you—and He doesn't make any junk." Caitlin's voice was firm. "When will you stop looking to people for approval? Their opinions don't matter a whit. It's God's opinion of you that really counts."

"I know you're right, Caity. And I do believe that, really. It's just that I guess I hadn't realized how much I'd changed since I left here ten years ago. I really do feel like I've earned my place here now."

"No, no, no! That's not it at all." Maryann shook her head, startling them with the loudness of her voice. "Sorry, I didn't mean to yell. But you haven't *earned* anything, Beth. You always belonged here.

If you feel more comfortable now, that's great, but you didn't have to leave and struggle for ten years, or get a degree, to be part of this town. You were always a part of it.''

"It didn't feel like I was." Beth hid the sting that those words caused. "I felt like an outsider who was unworthy. I had nothing to offer."

Caitlin shook her head vehemently. "Wrong. Honey, you're still holding on to this picture of yourself scraping and climbing to get out of the past, to reach your destiny. It simply isn't true."

"Isn't it? I was the local drunk's daughter. I had nothing to call my own. We starved half the time, and the rest of it we wondered where our next meal was coming from. How could Gar have married me then? I'd have ruined him." She closed her eyes and sighed, willing the ugly memories to recede. "And if I didn't spoil things, my father would have."

"And *that's* why you left." Caitlin nudged Maryann, whose eyes were also wide open in amazement. "You did it to save Gar from any indignity you thought he might suffer because of you or your father. I'm right, aren't I?"

Both women sat staring at her, demanding that she answer the question. When she could stand it no more, Beth finally nodded.

"Oh, you silly fool," Maryann scolded as she wrapped her arms around Beth. "I think you've caused yourself far more problems than your father ever could have."

"How can you say that? He was always showing up drunk." The embarrassment of it still shamed her, reddened her cheeks and made her want to run and hide.

"Listen to me, Beth. Drinking was your father's problem. If there's any shame to be borne, it is not yours. Nor are you any better because you got away from it. Your self-worth doesn't come from your father's binges any more than mine came from my parent's devotion to God." Maryann took her by the shoulders and forced her to look up and accept the truth shining in her eyes.

"She's right, Beth." Caitlin poured out more tea. "You've got to face this thing you have about your past and deal with it. It happened. You can't gloss over it or run away from it, or pretend you've risen above it. It will always be there. And maybe it did help shape who you are."

"But none of that has anything to do with your heart," Maryann continued, nodding at Caitlin in approval. "Your worth is built on God. You're His child and that makes you valuable, no matter whether you're as rich as Croesus or a ditchdigger. We don't think you're more worthy to be our friend because you've opened a business or earned a degree." Maryann squeezed her hand.

"Nor did we think any less of you when you told us the whole story about your past. We already knew the real Beth Ainslow, you see. She's a woman who cared enough about her sister to get her away from danger, to ensure her sister's safety at the expense of her own happiness." Tears formed at the end of Maryann's long lashes.

"She's also the woman who loved a man enough

to get out of his life rather than damage his chances for happiness. That's what you're worth, Beth. And it has absolutely nothing to do with how much you earn. We love you because you're you. Trust me, we wouldn't bother with just any old insecure pal." Caitlin laughed as she wrapped them both in her arms and hugged for all she was worth.

Beth indulged them in their group hug, but the questions still whirled around in her brain.

"It's been a long, hard road, but we're glad you're back here with us. Now, what about Gar?" Maryann was unrelenting.

"What about him? Nothing's really changed. We're still on totally separate courses. And we have nothing in common."

"You knock some sense into her, Caitlin. I give up! Anyone with two eyes could see that the two of them were meant to be together." Maryann stuck her nose in the air.

Caitlin shook her head slowly, her eyes pensive as they met Maryann's. "I don't think I can do that, Mare. This is something Beth needs to work out for herself. You and I will just have to pray that her eyes are opened."

"My eyes are wide open, Cait. And I can see exactly what would happen if Gar decided to pursue that political goal his father keeps dangling. In an electoral race, my past would come up, or I'd embarrass him somehow and he'd have to cover for me. I can't let that happen."

"Then why are you going to see his grandmother on Sunday?" Maryann demanded.

"Good question. Will you burst out laughing if I tell you I don't know why?" Beth murmured the words quietly, the admission weighing heavily on her mind. *Why am I spending more and more time with a man I'd vowed would have no part in my life?*

"There's hope for you yet, girlfriend." Something about the way Caitlin smiled as she leaned back in her armchair made Beth take a second look.

What did Caitlin know that she didn't?

"Gran, this is Beth Ainslow. Beth, I'd like you to meet my grandmother."

Beth took the porcelain hand carefully in hers. Mrs. Winthrop's skin looked like parchment that threatened to crack and fall to pieces if treated too roughly, but her grip was firm and sure. The tiny frail-looking woman fit in perfectly with the gingerbreadlike cottage in which she lived, but Beth suspected she was anything but delicate.

"My dear, how wonderful to meet you at last! I've heard so much about you. Do come in. I'm about to have some tea. You'll join me, of course."

"Oh. Thank you." Beth followed the tiny figure through to a cozy room filled with antiques covered in petit point. She chose the sturdiest looking chair and sat down on the edge, mindful of its delicate molded legs. "What, exactly, have you heard?"

"Wonderful things, dear. Just wonderful. My grandson can't say enough good things about you." She picked up the bone china teapot and poured three cups.

Beth's eyes opened wide as she digested this information. Gar talked about her to this woman? She studied him, hoping to see the topic of their discussions written across his lean face.

"Oh, not Garrett, dear. No, he's much too reserved for the kind of chitchat an old woman likes to hear. Tyler is the one who's been filling my head with your accomplishments. There you are."

Beth accepted the tea and sipped it carefully, fully aware that the china with its Limoges pattern was an heirloom and probably irreplaceable if she broke it.

"The boy seems quite infatuated with your sister."

"They get along very well. It's nice for Ronnie to have a friend."

They chatted desultorily back and forth for several minutes before Mrs. Winthrop spoke directly to Gar.

"I want to talk to this young lady alone, without you monitoring every word, Garrett. Why don't you take a walk?"

It was not a question, it was an order. Gar obeyed, though his eyes silently protested her decree. Minutes later he left the room, though he didn't bother to close the door.

"There, that's much better. Now tell me, my dear, will you be marrying Garrett soon?"

Beth stared at the twinkling blue eyes and swallowed hard. "We're not, uh, that is, Garrett and I aren't getting married." Strangely, it hurt to say those words out loud, and Beth didn't quite understand why. She was resigned to her new life, wasn't she?

"Really?" Mrs. Winthrop patted her silver-gray curls, her elegantly arched eyebrows rising. "Why not? You're in love, aren't you?"

"We were. Once. It was a long time ago."

"Yes, I know about that. You went away and married someone else. My grandson found that very hard to accept. He was so sure you loved him." The steel in those blue eyes wouldn't allow Beth to look away. "You did love him, didn't you?"

"Yes, I did. Very much."

"And something happened to change that. What was it, dear?"

The voice was compelling, daring her to lay it all out in the open. Beth resisted only a moment before deciding to pour out her heart. She related the past as quickly as possible.

"So you see, I didn't have any other choice. I had to go."

"Yes, I do see, Beth. I see quite clearly. But all that's in the past, and yet you still continue to see my grandson. Why is that, if not because of love?"

"I care for him very much, of course. But nothing much has changed. Gar is still an important person who feels called to do certain things. His world is far different from the world I'm in." Just saying it hurt immensely.

"All that claptrap is merely a shield to hide true feelings. Answer me, girl. Do you or do you not love my grandson?"

Beth couldn't look away from the determined

face, couldn't think of a way to avoid the probing questions. After several tense moments she nodded.

"Yes, I do. I think I love him more now than I did before."

Oh, the relief of saying that! The admission made her heart soar.

"It isn't his money you're attracted to?"

"Of course not! The money has nothing to do with it."

The periwinkle eyes darkened. "It did once, though, didn't it? I thought so." She nodded her head sagely, lips pursed. "Money and power, both used wrongly."

How did she know? Had her son told her? But no, Charles Winthrop had promised never to reveal that secret. Beth swallowed hard.

"I-I'm not sure what you mean." Beth hesitated, searching desperately for a way to avoid this discussion.

"Come now! You were eighteen, you had no money to pay rent or buy food. How could you have managed to get away from Oakburn unless someone helped you? If Garrett weren't head over heels in love with you, he'd have asked these questions long ago." Dinah Winthrop frowned. "It was my son, wasn't it? He bribed you to go."

"Not bribed, no." Beth let out a breath. "He simply explained the realities to me. Gar was in his first year. He had at least three more to go. And even when he was finished with college, money would be tight for us."

"And that's what decided it for you? The

money?'' A frown of dismay marred the delicate face.

''No. It wasn't the money.'' Beth allowed the shame of it to wash over her again. Even ten years later she felt totally humiliated by that awful scene. ''Your son and his wife invited me to their home one night. It was a wonderful evening. I had a new dress, and I felt like people were finally beginning to accept me for who I was, to accept that I was going to marry Gar.''

''Go on.'' The sweet gentle voice barely penetrated her musings.

''There were a lot of celebrities there, people your son knew and did business with. They came in limousines. The women wore jewels and expensive perfume. To me it was like a movie set.''

''Yes, Charles likes that sort of thing. I suppose it helps solidify his contacts in the business world, though you'd think he'd be beyond that egosoothing by now.''

''The mayors from three nearby cities had come also. I'd never seen anything like it. I was beginning to think the evening couldn't get any better, when Mr. Winthrop asked me to dance.'' She stopped, swallowing painfully. ''Then the dream cracked and broke into a thousand tiny pieces.''

The old woman merely waited, her bent fingers folded calmly in her lap. Her eyes glittered with some suppressed emotion, but she said nothing.

''My father somehow managed to elude the security people that night. He'd had more than his share of the drinks that were being served, and I guess that's what made him so bold. He accused Mr. Winthrop of causing my mother's death.''

"Was it true?''

"I don't know. I don't think so.'' Beth shook her head. "I don't remember much of what he said. All I remember is everyone staring at me, pitying me. He ranted and raved around the room, calling names and demanding that someone arrest your son. Then he turned on me.''

"Don't go over it again, dear. It must be very painful for you to remember.'' There were round spots of bright red color on the woman's cheeks.

"He turned on me, said I was degrading myself by hobnobbing with my mother's murderer.'' The words slipped out on their own accord, accompanied by a single teardrop. Beth stared at her hands, mortified.

"He said I was a nothing, a nobody who was trying to burrow her way into a place where I was out of my depth. That was when I realized that I didn't fit in and I never would. I wasn't the right kind of person. I didn't have the training or the social graces to brush that scene off and go on pretending that my father's diatribe meant nothing to me, or to anyone there.''

She swallowed hard. "It was true, you see. I was a nobody. And I had nothing to offer Gar. Nothing. I couldn't support him in his business because I didn't know anything about how that world worked. I came from the opposite side of the tracks, and nothing had prepared me for life in a place like Fairwinds.''

"And?"

"I was worried about my past harming the man I loved. What if Dad had said those things in front of Gar—condemned him the same way he condemned me?"

The cuckoo clock in the corner called out four o'clock as a log hissed sparks in the fireplace. But other than that, the room was broodingly silent.

"I couldn't put him through it. I couldn't ask him to put up with all that hate, all that blame. I couldn't rake over the past, especially when your son told me that he'd been the one to turn down my mother's plea for help the day she died." The tears flowed unchecked now.

"It was just a business decision. It wasn't personal. I understood that. But my dad had made it into some kind of vendetta, and he wouldn't stop his accusations, no matter how many times Mr. Winthrop offered to give him a new loan." She gulped. "The whole place was buzzing with the gossip."

The old lady's lips were tight with reproof now. Her fingers grasped the arms of her chair tightly, clearly outlining the blue veins on her hands.

"My mother had been gone for some time. I didn't care about the past, but I knew there was something I could do about the future. When my father's drunken absences got longer, and conditions at home grew much worse, I decided to go away— to leave before Ronnie got caught in the awful mess."

"That was a very smart, brave thing to do. It can't have been easy."

"Actually, it was." Beth smiled, dashing away her tears. "Mr. Winthrop came to see me. He explained that he felt it would be best if I went away for a while, got some training. I could come back, later on, when he'd smoothed things over. Gar was going to be tied up with college anyway, so why not prepare myself for when he came back. I let your son believe that I would be back someday when I told him I was taking Ronnie and leaving Oakburn to look for a job."

"And Charles gave you money, didn't he."

Beth nodded. "A loan, yes. He said he'd wished hundreds of times that he'd given it to my mother, lent a hand when it would have done some good. Since he couldn't help her, he'd help me."

"You took it." It wasn't a question. The old lady's eyes were fixed on the blue chintz love seat across the room.

"I took it and promised to pay him back. I gave him a letter for Gar, and I left town before the gossip got even more unbearable. A few months later I met a wonderful man, a man who fell in love with me—the real me. He wanted to marry me, to take care of Ronnie." Beth smiled, remembering that strange proposal.

"What was he like?"

"Denis was a lot like me, I guess. He'd grown up poor, worked his way up through the ranks until he built himself a reputation on the oil rigs. He was good and solid and dependable, and I knew he would never let me down. I didn't have to pretend around Denis. I could relax and be myself."

"You loved him?" The voice broke through her reverie.

"He was my friend, my advisor, my comforter, my partner in raising Ronnie. After a while I think I did grow to love him, but in a different way than I loved Gar. There wasn't any excitement or razzle-dazzle, not the way there is when I'm near Gar." She squinted, wondering if she'd offended this regal old woman. "Do you know what I mean?"

Mrs. Winthrop smiled, nodding. "I certainly do, my dear. And razzle-dazzle is a perfect description. It's the way my dear husband made me feel, too. Anything else is second best."

"I suppose. But I didn't feel like that about Denis. He was just—" Beth frowned, thinking it over "—Comfortable is the right word, I guess."

"What will you do now?"

"Go on building my business and seeing Ronnie through school." Why did that sound so bleak and unfulfilling?

"I understand she's a very bright girl. You've done well."

"Yes, Ronnie's far smarter than I ever was. And I mean for her to make something of herself. I don't want her to ever feel as inferior as I did. I want her to be strong and secure."

Not that anyone could possibly believe Ronnie would ever be unsure of herself. The girl was comfortable wherever she went. *At least I've done that for her.*

"That's commendable, my dear. And I'm sure

your sister will be fine. But aren't you putting an awful burden on her as well?''

Beth frowned. "I don't know what you mean."

Dinah Winthrop smiled as she picked up the poker and stabbed the glowing logs to new life. Her actions sent up a sheet of sparks that spooked the cat lying on the mantel.

"You're projecting your own wishes on her in exactly the same manner that my son projects his will on his children. Haven't you noticed?"

Beth shook her head. "No, not at all. Mr. Winthrop wanted Garrett to go into banking, of course. But that was what Gar wanted, too."

"Yes, Garrett was more malleable than Tyler, I'm afraid. He let himself be made into a carbon copy of his father—"

"I don't think that's quite accurate, Grandmother." Gar strolled into the room, his words echoing off the plaster ceiling. Both women started in surprise. "I am *nothing* like my father, and what I've heard just proves it. I would never turn away a woman desperately searching for help for her family." His tones were measured. But his eyes blazed with anger as they lighted on Beth. "Why didn't you tell me?"

"H-how much did you hear?"

"All of it, I hope. I'm not all that obedient when it comes to being shooed out of the room like a naughty little boy. When I came back from speaking with Cook, you were talking about leaving town. I always wondered why you'd left, Beth. I don't know why I didn't guess that you'd had help." He shifted from one foot to the other, hands clenched at his sides.

"I never wanted you to know about it." A tide of red burned Beth's cheeks as she realized how much she'd given away. Had he heard her profess her love?

"Just to set the record straight, I never got any letter."

"But you must have!" Beth stared at him, trying to assimilate this new information. "I specifically asked your father to give it to you the next time you came home."

"I didn't come home for quite a long time, Beth. I learned about your departure a week before Christmas break. A friend wondered why I hadn't gone home to say goodbye." He smiled grimly. "I called and called but you weren't there. Father or no father, I made up my mind right then to find you. I was out of school for six months, searching for some information, some thread that would have led me to you. I couldn't find a thing. You hid yourself well, Beth."

"You looked for me?" She couldn't believe what he was saying.

"Of course. You didn't think I'd just let you go, did you?" His face tightened, lines of fury radiating from his eyes.

"Yes, I did." Beth nodded, then swallowed when his face grew darker. "I hoped you'd understand from the letter that I wasn't right for you, that I couldn't change myself into that kind of person."

"I didn't want you to change! I liked you the way

you were. Are. Whatever. And may I repeat that I *did not* get any letter.'' He bellowed the words, and then instantly offered his grandmother an apology. ''I'm sorry, Gran. You don't need to hear all this.''

''On the contrary, dear boy, I'd like to hear even more. The situation has bothered me for some time.'' She refolded her hands in her lap and smiled. ''Go on.''

''I don't really think we should air our problems in front of your grandmother,'' Beth protested. ''I'm sure she'd like some peace and quiet.''

''No, she wouldn't.'' Gar's voice was firm. ''Dinah thrives on people. And even though she's supposed to live quietly nowadays, she never does what the doctors say. So stop using her as an excuse.''

Beth straightened her shoulders, affronted. ''I do not require an excuse. We weren't even properly engaged, if you recall, Garrett Winthrop. You said we'd do it up right when you graduated.''

His eyes opened wide. ''I proposed, you accepted. I even gave you a promise ring. In my books that's called being engaged. The time line doesn't have a thing to do with it.'' He stood in front of her, arms folded across his chest in a belligerent attitude that spoke volumes.

''Oh, you make me so angry sometimes! Don't bother acting so hoity-toity with me, Gar. I know very well that you were dating other girls in college. And you found one especially attractive, didn't you? I believe her name was Carric. And now there's Cynthia.'' Beth flopped back onto her chair with a huff, her face hot.

"I am *not* dating Cynthia Reardon. If one more person tells me I am, I'll..."

"You'll what?" Beth demanded. "Did you ever stop to think that everyone is saying it because they believe it's the truth?"

"Just like they believed you ran away because you were pregnant? I suppose I'm to blame for that erroneous conclusion, too?" As soon as he said it, Gar groaned and slapped a hand to his head. "I'm sorry, Beth. You're the only person I know who can make me say things I shouldn't."

Beth stared at him. "They thought I was pregnant?" She couldn't take it in, couldn't absorb what he was saying. "They thought that you and I...that we had...oh no!" She closed her eyes and wept. "The talk that must have gone around. And you were here through it all."

"I'm tough, I managed." He smiled softly. "And anyway, who cares about the talk, Beth? It doesn't matter. Don't you see that yet?" Gar knelt in front of her, his big warm hands covering hers. "What we need to get at is the truth. All of it, no matter how much it hurts. Okay?"

She nodded.

"And I'm going to go first." He got up, hooked a chair over and sat down in front of her, his face inches from hers.

"I wasn't going out with anyone, Beth. Sure, groups of us went out for coffee sometimes, but there was never anyone special. You had my heart. Carrie was just a friend."

"That's why you invited her to your graduation?

My dad told me that when I telephoned one night,'' she added at his raised brow. ''It was *our* dream, Gar. Ours. And you shared it with her.''

''Because you weren't there to share it with, and I was lonely. Don't you see? I waited, I even looked for you that day. But you never came.''

''I was there,'' she whispered. ''You didn't see me, but I was there. In my heart. I even wished you congratulations.''

He sat silently, staring into her eyes for a long time. Then slowly, gradually, a smile started in his eyes and worked its way down to his mouth.

''Congratulations to you, too. I guess you noticed I wasn't at yours, either.''

She allowed herself time just to stare at him, to absorb the wonder of a love that—no matter how hard she tried to believe otherwise—had never really died. A love that couldn't be killed no matter how much she told herself she didn't care anymore.

''So what now?'' It was Dinah's voice, brimming with laughter as she sat perched in her chair. ''Where do we go from here?''

''I don't know.'' Gar turned from scrutinizing his grandmother to Beth, his eyes asking a question she was afraid to answer.

''I don't know, either. I have to rethink it all, reevaluate what I've learned. Nothing is as it seemed.'' Beth shook her head, hoping to clear it. But nothing could dislodge what she thought she saw burning deep in Gar's eyes.

Did he still love her? She didn't know. But until

she did, she wasn't making any life-altering decisions. Not again.

"Nothing is the same, you're right. Things are better. We've cleared the air between us. But I think we deserve to hear the whole story. And there are two men who can explain it to us." Gar surged to his feet, planted a hearty kiss on his grandmother's cheek and grabbed Beth's hand.

"Thanks for tea, Gran. But we have to go now. There's someone—actually two someones—we need to talk to."

A shiver of fear trickled down her spine as Beth rose to follow him.

The truth was about to come out. Why was she so afraid?

# Chapter Eight

"Beth and I would like to talk to you about the past, Dad. Alone." A hardness tinged the melodic timbre of Gar's low voice.

Ty and Ronnie glanced up from the puzzle they were assembling. Beth could see the questions on both their faces. She wanted to tell them not to worry, to get on with their own lives. She longed to do that herself. But she couldn't. She and Gar couldn't move ahead until the past was straightened out.

"I'm sure the children won't mind if we talk here." Charles's voice was amiable enough, but there were frown lines on his forehead and his now-whitened cheeks.

"I don't think you want that, do you, Dad?" Gar stared hard at his father and only slightly relaxed when Mr. Winthrop finally got to his feet. "Let's go to the study."

Two minutes later Beth was ushered to a wine-colored chair that sat in front of a huge desk. Nervously, she folded her hands in her lap, then unfolded them and laid her fingers out straight. She knew Gar was furious. He hadn't said a word all the way here, other than to ask her politely if she was all right or needed the heat turned up.

In truth, Beth felt icy cold when she saw the way his gray eyes glittered. She glanced at him now, noting the way he sat in his own chair, his back straight, his shoulders rigid. The truth had to come out, but at what cost? Would it drive a wedge between the two who had always been so close?

"I want to know everything. And I'm not going to stop asking until I get the truth. No games, Dad. That's gone on for years now. I think that's quite long enough."

"You can't fault me for doing what I thought best." Charles sat behind the desk, leaning back in his chair as if he were afraid Gar would lunge at him.

Beth found it interesting that he didn't even pretend not to know what they were talking about.

"Best for whom? Me? Beth? Best for Mervyn? Just who were you helping by paying Beth to leave town?"

"I didn't pay her." Charles sputtered indignantly at such a description. "I merely made her a loan."

A nasty smile tightened Gar's mouth. "I'm sure you did. And probably collected interest. Am I right?" He glanced over at Beth, inclining his head a bit when she nodded.

"Of course I'm right! That's the whole reason for this family, isn't it, Dad? We've got to make more and more money. Doesn't matter at whose expense."

"Now just a minute, son. She had to leave. Mervyn was getting worse. He disappeared for days sometimes. That's no environment for a child!"

Beth glanced at Gar. He was so hurt. He'd never suspected his father of doing anything this underhanded. How difficult it must be to find out the truth this way.

"No way at all for young girls to live." The younger Winthrop agreed, a hint of a smile touching his angry lips. "And, of course, you did everything in your power to help Beth and Veronica, didn't you? I mean, you saw to it that someone took over some groceries, made sure the pastor looked out for them, even sent a friend after Mervyn to make sure he didn't hurt himself. Well, didn't you?"

Charles looked at the floor, his hand clenched by his side.

"No, I didn't think so. You looked the other way instead. It's so hard to see children starving, isn't it, Dad? Kind of eats away at you." Gar surged to his feet and strode around the room, his hands thrust into his pockets.

Though Beth ached for him, she couldn't think of a thing to say that would make any of this easier to swallow. So she sat where she was and whispered a prayer that this relationship between father and son wouldn't be totally ruined by the past.

"Son, I don't think they were starving. They always seemed healthy enough to me."

"Don't you dare call me 'son'! Right now I'm so ashamed of you, I'm almost sick to my stomach. How would you know how the girls managed? You never bothered to find out. Is that what happened when Beth's mother came to you for a loan? You turned away and focused on other things?"

What little color was left in the old man's face now drained completely away, leaving him gray and shriveled.

"How did you—"

"'Be sure your sin will find you out.' Isn't that what you've always preached to me, Dad? I guess yours have come home to roost, haven't they?" He smiled grimly. "What did you say to Mrs. Ainslow that made her so despondent she didn't check the intersection for oncoming cars?"

Beth frowned. How had he known how her mother died? Gar hadn't been any older than she.

"I couldn't grant that loan, Garrett! She had nothing, *nothing* to back it. We had a lot of shareholders back then, folks who depended on the bank for their income. I was responsible to them and to my own family to be sure the bank was covered."

"The bank? The bank is made up of people. Human beings whose lives are more important than earning another few dollars!" Gar glared at his father, his face tight with strain. Only his eyes burned. "You know Grandfather's edict as well as I. 'Whenever possible, help.' How could you let her just walk away?"

Charles Winthrop bowed his head, his hands fidgeting in his lap. When he finally looked up, there were tears in his eyes—eyes that begged for understanding.

"I've gone over it a thousand times in my mind. And I've wished ten thousand times that I could change the past. But I can't. I couldn't then and I can't now." The thin shoulders slumped as the old man admitted his mistake. "I knew Mervyn was right. I killed Loretta Ainslow as surely as if I'd pushed her into that street." He looked up at Beth, his face drawn and haggard now. "I'm sorry, Beth. So sorry."

A well of forgiveness opened inside her at the sight of that pitiable man. He'd made a wrong choice and it had cost him years of pain. Why continue adding to it now? What difference would it make to anyone?

"It doesn't matter now," she whispered softly, leaning forward to cradle his cold, blue-veined hand in her own. "It's in the past."

"How can you say it doesn't matter?" Gar blasted his barely concealed indignation at her words, his voice seething with hurt as he raged at the injustice.

His words hit Beth with a fierceness that shocked her, yet drew her nearer. She felt a tender sympathy for both men—Charles because he had to live with his consequences, and Gar because it hurt to see how imperfect a parent could be. His pain was at least partly on her account, and she felt cherished. She sat silently as he continued.

"All right, he made a mistake with your mother. But he didn't learn a thing, no matter how guilty that mistake made him feel." He turned back to his father and demanded, "How could you do it all over again with the woman I loved?"

The anguish in those bitter challenges ate at Beth like acid, as Gar audibly agonized over his father's perfidy. She wanted to go to him, hold him close and promise that she would soothe away the hurt. But Gar was not a child, and the anger festering inside needed to be let out. She could only watch and listen. And pray for him.

For them both.

"You knew how much I loved Beth. You watched me hunt for her. I begged you a hundred times to hire a private investigator but you refused. And all the time *you* were the one who had sent her away, convinced her that the money mattered more than the love. How could you do that, *Dad*?" The sarcasm in the last word was unmistakable.

"I was doing what I thought was best." Charles gave Beth an apologetic glance. "I mean no disrespect, my dear, but you were not our kind. That was evident at the party. You had no knowledge of the industry, and even less as hostess. You were afraid of your own shadow, and there were those who would have been happy to decry both you and my son."

"Our kind? What is 'our kind,' Dad?" Gar's scathing voice made a mockery of the apology. "Because if 'our kind' means lying and cheating and even stealing, then I'm proud to say I'm not 'our kind' either.''

''Stealing?'' Charles huffed up, indignant at the accusation. ''I've never stolen anything.''

''You stole a letter that was addressed to me from Beth. You promised her that you'd give it to me and then you lied to me, the son you profess to love. You cheated us out of ten years when we could have been together, happy. Explain that, *Dad*.''

Charles hung his head. ''I destroyed that letter as soon as she left town. I couldn't allow you to stop your education.''

''You couldn't 'allow' it? What right did you have? Certainly not the right of a loving father.''

Beth had always wondered at the term ''broken man.'' But that was exactly what Charles Winthrop was now. Broken and bent as Gar heaped accusation after accusation on his head. Ill and elderly, the arrogant man seemed a mere shadow.

''That's enough, Garrett.'' Beth stood and walked over to the tea cart. She poured out a tumbler of water and held it to the old man's lips while he took a sip. ''You've asked your questions, gotten your answers, laid down your judgments. Now leave it alone. You're not helping anyone with all this anger.'' She smiled at the old man, patted his shoulder, then returned the cup to the tray.

Gar grabbed her arm, his face a contorted mask of questions that demanded answers.

''What? How can you say that? He spoiled our lives!''

She shook her head, studying this man in a whole

new light. "No, he didn't. Oh, maybe he helped make things more difficult, just as my father did." She thought about that time as a wry smile lifted her lips. "But the truth is that you and I spoiled our own lives."

"*I* didn't spoil anything." Gar flopped down on the sofa, obviously disgruntled by her lack of support.

"Yes, you did. If you'd come home when I begged you to, if you'd listened to what I had to say, we could have talked things through. But you didn't. You were too busy playing Romeo." She laughed, in hindsight, at the silliness of it all. "And I was a fool to leave without forcing you to listen to my explanation. I let all my doubts and fears take over. I didn't trust you enough. I didn't trust God enough, so I made my own solution."

"Yeah, some solution. Marrying Denis."

The sour look on Gar's face sank in as Beth realized exactly why he had always decried her husband. He was jealous. She walked over to stand in front of him.

"Funny you should think Denis was the wrong solution. That's the one part of this whole debacle that I'm almost positive must have come directly from God. I needed someone strong, someone who could teach me to rely on God and myself. Denis was that man." She smiled, her hand gentle as it brushed through Gar's spiky hair.

"Marrying Denis didn't mean that I loved you any less, Garrett. I've always loved you. Maybe more now than ever before. You're a part of me. That could never die."

He stood and wrapped his arms around her waist, tugging her closer to his heart. His eyes glowed with a fierceness that sent a thrill of wonder through her.

"Do you mean it? Really, Beth? You still love me?"

She nodded, her eyes welling with tears of joy. "I really mean it."

"I love you, Beth. And I *am* going to marry you. Maybe it's ten years late, but there is a wedding on the way." He leaned around her to glare at his father. "And there's nothing you can do to stop it."

Charles Winthrop got up slowly, his body stooped. He walked around the desk slowly, holding the edge for support. But when he looked at his son, there was a warmth, love and deep compassion in his eyes that Beth understood.

"On the contrary, Garrett. I'm going to do everything in my power to speed it through. As soon as possible. I wish you both the very best."

Beth slipped out of Gar's arms and stepped over to the old man. "Thank you," she whispered as she kissed his paper-thin cheek. "For understanding."

His eyes met hers, questioning. Beth smiled and patted the thin hand.

"He'll come around. I'll make sure of it. Just takes a little time."

"Thank *you*, my dear. I don't deserve it, but I'm grateful for your forgiveness."

There wasn't anything she could say to that in front of Gar, so Beth merely smiled.

"I'll go tell the children the good news. I have a hunch it won't come as a surprise. They've been planning something like this for a while." Charles pulled open the door and then stopped. "Besides, I've a little something to discuss with Tyler. The boy's grades are dropping every semester."

"Now that we've had our showdown, I guess my little brother's going to have to face the music." Gar stood behind Beth, his arms closing around her waist. "It's about time, too. He's been dragging his heels long enough."

Beth turned and placed a finger on his lips. "Forget about Tyler," she murmured, her eyes taking in every detail of his handsome face. "Did you just propose to me, Garrett Winthrop?"

"Yes. And no matter what you try, this time it's going to happen. I suggest Valentine's Day. Does that give you enough time?" His lips nuzzled her cheek in a tender caress.

"I don't need much time, just enough to talk to my dad."

Gar frowned. "Are you sure you want to? I mean, it might end up hurting you if he can't get past his bitterness."

Beth hugged him close, her head against his heart. "Then that's a choice he'll have to make. I can't make it for him. I finally realized that I do care for him, but it's time he faced up to his part in our awful past."

"But it is the past, isn't it? It's not going to interfere with our future?" The anxious note in his voice and the frown on his face ushered out the last doubt that had lingered in her mind.

Gar loved her. She loved him. What else did they need?

Gar followed Beth into the nursing home with doubts plaguing every step. He wasn't positive this was a good idea. Mervyn had carried his grudge for a long time. It wouldn't be easy to let it go.

"Stop mincing along! He's not going to bite you." Beth shook her head in disgust, then wrapped an arm through Gar's. "I'll defend you if he does. Or dress your wound. How's that?"

"Not very comforting," Gar muttered, and pushed open the door to Mervyn's room.

"Hi, Dad. How are you today?" The forced cheeriness in Beth's voice was evident.

"Same as yesterday. Probably the same as to-morrow. Not that you care."

"Of course I care. I always have, in spite of the way I acted. That's why I'm here to see you today." Beth sank into a chair near her father's and explained what they'd learned this afternoon. "I guess the end result is that Gar and I still love one another and we intend to be married. On Valentine's Day."

"What? You're allying yourself with the son of the man who killed your mother?" Mervyn snorted in disgust as an angry red flush suffused his face. "How can you do that?"

"I can marry Gar because I love him. Just as I loved him ten years ago. Only more so now." She winked at Gar, her fingers reaching for his.

Gar squeezed her hand but stayed where he was, leaning against the wall. He wanted to be prepared for whatever Mervyn tried to pull. Something told him this wouldn't be a pretty scene.

"You have no idea of the pain that family has put us through." Beth's father glared at them both.

"Yes, Dad. I do. But it's a pain you also contributed to."

"Me?" Mervyn coughed in amazement, his eyes wide. "I did nothing."

"Exactly." Beth sat back in her chair as if she were lounging, but Gar could tell she was strengthening herself for what was to come. "Why did Mother go to the bank that day, Dad? You'd had an argument the night before, I remember. Did her trip have anything to do with your disagreement or the fact that you were off on a bender when she was killed?"

Flustered and indignant, Mervyn's mouth opened and closed several times like that of a fish gulping water. If it hadn't been so sad, it would have been comical. Gar watched the man fidget in his seat, and swallowed down his anger. There were elements of a tragedy in his past, but he had moments, good moments, to remind him of the way things could be with his dad.

The real tragedy was that a relationship had never been allowed to develop between this father and his daughters.

"You're acting just like the Winthrops now, girl. That figures!" The words were sharp, but it was just a show, a shallow pretense.

"Did Mom go to ask the bank for some money so she could buy some food, Dad? Or maybe she needed that money you spent on your drinking buddies to pay for those pills she had to take." Anger glittered in Beth's green eyes as she thrust her head back. Her hair blazed reddish-gold. "Did you drink away my mother's life that afternoon?"

"You're just like her, Bethy. Her gold hair got full of those red-colored sparks when she was mad, too. Boy, did she have a temper." Mervyn's eyes glazed over with memories. "She stood up for what she believed and she never took 'no' for an answer. She was determined to take that job over in Moss Creek, and if it meant we had to get a car, she was going to get it. Nothing could have stopped her."

"But she had a job. She cleaned at the bank." Beth glanced at Gar, but he shrugged.

He had no idea what had happened all those years ago, except that Mrs. Ainslow had been hit by a vehicle while crossing the intersection. But he intended to find out the truth now. And then, please God, they could finally put it all behind them.

"She wanted something better than I could provide. She was determined that you girls wouldn't suffer because of us and the problems we had. So she went to *his* father to ask for four hundred lousy dollars to buy that car. A pittance!" Mervyn glared at Gar, malevolence on his face.

"But that wasn't good enough for his old man. No, he had to humiliate her further by reminding her that we were behind on the loans we already had."

"I'm guessing that she had no idea how deeply you were in debt. Right, Dad?" Beth didn't wait for a nod. The look on Mervyn's face said it all. "How can you blame this on someone else? How can you act as if it's not just as much your fault? You pushed her into that humiliation by drinking away every dime she hid in that old tin coffee can."

Mervyn stared. "How did you—"

"Oh, don't worry, Dad. She covered for you. But I wasn't stupid. I knew what was going on. When she thought we were asleep she'd start crying. Did you know that, Dad? She'd pray a little prayer over and over. 'Please, God, take care of my babies.' Then she'd start that awful coughing." Beth chewed on her bottom lip as she fought for control.

"I'm sorry, Bethy. I'm so sorry." That broken voice tugged at Gar's heartstrings.

But Beth wasn't in a forgiving mood. "You weren't one bit sorry. Don't you see? If you had been sorry, you would have thrown away that bottle and knuckled down to taking care of us after she died. We could have consoled each other. Instead, you got your consolation in an alcohol-induced haze that lasted just long enough for me to have to stay up all night, worrying if you were ever coming home." She burst into tears then, great racking sobs that tore at her thin body.

Gar would have gone to her then, taken her in his arms and consoled her. Even physically removed her from the room. But the look in her eyes held him back, so he stayed where he was, chafing at the inner voice that told him to keep still while she bared her soul.

"Do you know what my memories are of the time after Mom died? What would we eat? How could I make sure Ronnie would be okay? Were you going to go away and leave us again? Every day. All day. All night." She stood and dashed the tears from her face, her eyes raging.

"You're not sorry in the least, Dad. You're still doing the same thing to me today, using me or the Winthrops or anybody else who's handy to justify a situation you created. Even now you play Ronnie off against me, blame me for taking her away, and fill her head with stories that have no relationship to our ugly reality."

"You took her away from me. My own little girl." His voice cracked. "I wanted to protect my wife, make things right for her. Just like I want to make sure you and Ronnie are okay."

Mervyn stretched out a hand, which Beth ignored. Gar watched as the old man pulled open a desk drawer and took out a small flask. Gar knew exactly what was inside, and he saw by the look in her eyes that Beth did, too.

"Yes, I can see how badly you want that," she scoffed. "You'll blank me out, make all the bad stuff disappear. For a little while, anyway. And Ronnie and I will be left to deal with the pieces, the scandal and the dubious distinction of being known as the town drunk's daughters. Thanks a lot, Dad."

As Gar watched, Beth stormed out of the room, tears pouring down her white cheeks. He wanted to follow her, but some little voice inside told him to stay.

Mervyn sat where he was, stunned by the words that she had thrown at him.

"I failed her, didn't I?" The old man stared at his hands.

"We all did, Mervyn. Me, Dad, you. We should have been there for her, but we weren't. And in spite of everything, she managed to take care of herself and raise Ronnie." He smiled gently, holding out his handkerchief for the old man to use. "That's quite a daughter you have."

"She looks exactly like her mother. It used to make me crazy when I'd come home from work and she'd be standing there with those great big eyes in that heart-shaped face. I missed Loretta so much, but everywhere I turned, there was another reminder of her in Beth." He lifted the flask to his lips as if to take another sip.

Gar reached out and stopped him, knowing this was the last chance Mervyn would get to alter a pattern that had developed years ago between himself and his children.

"Do you love your kids, Mr. Ainslow?"

Mervyn frowned, but at least he lowered the flask from his lips. "Of course I love them. They're all I have left."

"You're going to lose them." Gar paused, letting his words sink in. "Beth gave up everything to come back here because Ronnie wanted to get to know you again. Your eldest daughter kept her sister away as long as she could, carried the stigma of your failures on her shoulders and kept your misdeeds to herself so her little sister could grow up free and happy.''

He picked the flask out of the wrinkled hand and set it on the table. Then he put the girls' pictures on the table beside it. ''You start drinking again and you're going to lose them both. For good.''

The tired eyes flashed with anger, but Gar ignored that. He was fighting for his future happiness. And Beth's. He wouldn't give up easily.

''Beth and I are getting married, and there is nothing you or anyone else can do to prevent that. But I'm only too well aware of how much your behavior has shamed her, how she's covered up for you, lied when you disappeared on one of your binges, taken over your role as father when she needed a father herself.''

''Hah!'' Mervyn's hand reached out to grab the flask, but Gar stopped him. ''What do you know?''

''I know this. If you begin drinking again, I will take Beth away from here, and Ronnie will come with us—after she's been told the truth. You will never see either one of your daughters again. This is your last chance to be a father, Mervyn. Your children or your bottle. Choose.''

''You don't understand!'' The pathetically sad face made Gar squirm. ''I have these dreams. I'm sure Loretta is here. I reach out and I almost touch her and *whoosh*—it's gone. Then I remember. And it hurts.'' His voice was tortured, proof that he still yearned for what he couldn't have.

But Gar remained undeterred. There were two

lovely young women who desperately needed to know that their father cared about them. He was fighting for that.

"I know all about your dream, Mervyn. I've had the same one for the last ten years." He swallowed hard, forcing himself to continue. "It's my wedding day. I'm at the church, at the front, waiting for Beth to walk down that aisle. The music starts, the congregation stands, and I know it's finally going to happen. Then I wake up and I'm alone. Still." He smiled grimly. "Believe me, I know about that kind of longing."

Gar moved to the window and stared out at the glistening white snow that shone in the moon's bright glow. He thought about the agonizing that always followed those awful dreams.

"The thing is, God's given us both a second chance, if we want to take it. I intend to make my dream a reality. I am going to marry Beth." He turned to face his future father-in-law.

Mervyn sat there, morose and frowning, but his attention was on Gar.

"What about you? Are you finally going to build a family, or are you going to throw it all away for a lousy drink that will only dull the truth for a little while? Is this bottle what you want for a family? Last chance, Mervyn. Decide."

The clock ticked away the minutes, one by one, as Gar forced himself to keep his eyes focused on the man in front of him. There would be time for Beth and him later, he was confident of that. But there might never be another time to reach Mervyn

Ainslow, to give Beth back the father she longed for but was afraid to trust. He waited, silently praying.

With slow, hesitant movements, Mervyn got to his feet. He picked up the flask and clutched it tightly in his hand. Gar felt his heart sink to his feet.

*Oh, God, why? Why can't You heal this hurting family?*

He closed his eyes and prayed harder than he ever remembered praying.

"You might be marrying her, but she's still my daughter." Mervyn stood at the sink, allowing the amber liquid to dribble from the glass bottle into the sink and down the drain. "And that will never change."

*Thank you, God!*

"Gar?" Beth stepped inside the room, rubbing her hands up and down her arms. She refused to look at her father. "I'm freezing. If you're going to stay here a while, I'll walk home."

"Bethy?" Mervyn stood where he was, still holding his flask over the sink. When she turned to glare at him, he let the bottle drop and faced her, his eyes moist.

Gar saw a flicker of hope in her eyes as she glanced from her father's hand to the sink and back again.

"I'm sorry, Bethy. I've failed you and Ronnie so badly. It would serve me right if you never came here again." Mervyn swallowed hard, then took a step forward. His face was sallow.

"I've been a lousy husband and father. I know

that. But if you'll let me, I promise I'll try to change.''

"You've said that before," she muttered, averting her eyes to stare at the floor.

"And then I went on another bender. I know. I embarrassed you at that party and I felt so bad, I just wanted to disappear." Mervyn gulped. "When I looked at you, I saw her. And that hurt something fierce. I wanted her back."

"But instead I was there, demanding you be a father to Ronnie and me," Beth whispered. Her eyes were dark, glistening with unshed tears.

"I had to lash out, I was so angry. And then I had to get away. I couldn't stay there and see you and not be reminded of how much I loved Loretta, and of how badly I failed her. And you. It hurt too much." The poignant words trailed away.

A long silence hung between father and daughter as they stared into each other's eyes. As Gar watched the wordless communication, he prayed.

"You can't run away anymore, Dad. We don't have that much time to waste. If you want to be our father, it's got to start now. Ronnie needs you."

Mervyn nodded, but his eyes were intently studying the young girl who'd grown into a woman. Gar had a feeling that the old man was finally seeing the beautiful woman who stood before him as herself, his own dear daughter—not some dream-like replica of her long-dead mother.

"And you?" Mervyn's voice was stronger now. "What about you, Beth? What do you want?"

"The past is finished, done." The corners of her

wide mouth tipped up in a wry grin. "And to tell you the truth, after today I don't care if I never hear about it again. I want the future. With Gar. And you. I want Ronnie to be proud of you, to know you as I remember you—before the drinking." There were tears now, but they were hopeful tears.

"And?" Mervyn stood where he was, waiting.

Beth gulped down a sob. "I want you to walk me down the aisle when I marry Gar. I want my family to be there for me."

"I'll be there." Mervyn's voice sounded rusty; it squeaked in places. "I promise you, Beth. I'll be there, stone-cold sober."

At last Beth flew into her father's embrace, her sobs joyful at this reunion with the man whose memory had haunted her for years.

As he watched them hold each other, Gar heaved a sigh of relief. *Thank you, God.*

Now, if they could just get on with the wedding!

# Chapter Nine

The ride home was slower than it needed to be because Gar took a detour. Beth didn't mind. She basked in her father's words and reveled in the thrill of having Gar's arm around her shoulders, snuggling her as close as they could get with the stick shift between them.

"Where are we going?" she asked, glancing around and seeing nothing familiar.

"I'm abducting you. And it's a secret hideout, so close your eyes."

Beth complied, content to let the pictures waft through her mind. *A wedding.* Two days ago she wouldn't have dreamed this was possible, and now suddenly she was positive it would happen, perhaps sooner than anyone imagined.

"Keep your eyes closed now."

"They're closed already! What is this all about, anyway?"

"You'll see."

She was aware that the car had stopped, felt Gar move, and then shivered as a gust of cold air rushed in when her own door was opened. Moments later she felt herself being lifted out of the car. She giggled at the strange feeling of being carried who knew where. She clasped both arms around his neck, relaxed and enjoyed it.

"What are you doing with me?" she demanded.

"I'm ensuring that for once in this relationship, we have some privacy," he told her. "You can open your eyes now."

Beth did so, and glanced around, startled by the beauty of the room she'd just entered. She slid to her feet, taking in the lustrously polished cedar walls, the stone fireplace and the soaring ceilings. A glance out the window showed they were somewhere out of town, but she couldn't see much except for the snow-covered hills that gleamed under a full moon.

"Where is this?"

"This is our home. Or at least, I hope it will be. I built it a few years ago in the hope that when you finally came back, you'd live here with me. I haven't stayed here much, though." He looked sheepish. "I never told you this, but I've been waiting for you to come home. I've had this dream of you here."

Come home? Had she really? Beth touched a hand to his cheek and stared into his eyes. She smiled and nodded, finally willing to accept that anywhere with Gar would be home. Things didn't matter.

After several solemn moments, Gar moved toward the fireplace and lit the little pile of paper and kindling that lay waiting. When the fire grew stronger he added more and more sticks until it was a well-established blaze. Then he rose, dusted off his knees and walked back toward her, stopping once beside a big chest. Beth heard him open a drawer, but was too busy looking around the beautiful room to pay any attention.

"Come on, Beth. Sit down." He ushered her to the big golden sofa, and, when she'd sunk into its softness, he knelt in front of her. "I have something I want to say."

"Okay." She loved him, she wanted to marry him, to live here with him. So why did this all feel so strange?

"I've been in love with you for years, Beth Ainslow. There have been times, lots of them, when I've wondered if you would ever come to this place. And I promised myself that if you did, I'd do this properly." He stared into her eyes, his own glowing dark with suppressed emotions.

"I love you. I always will. I finally realized that I don't care about the past anymore. My focus is on the future." One hand picked up hers, squeezing it gently. "Will you please marry me, Beth?"

She couldn't hold back—a "yes" burst out of her, heartfelt and confident. She saw his smile of satisfaction, then noticed the ring he was holding out.

"This was my grandmother's, given to her by her husband when my dad was born. The stone was a very rare find by a man they'd loaned money to when they didn't have much to loan. Grandfather asked him to keep the stone until he could afford to buy it, and his friend agreed. It took him almost ten years, but he finally bought it on the day my dad was born. He said they'd waited so long to have children, he wanted to commemorate God's goodness.''

"What a lovely history!"

"Dinah gave it to me several years ago and told me I should only give it to the one woman I wanted to share the rest of my life with. Will you wear it until we can get a proper engagement ring?"

The unusual garnet glowed with a rich yellow-green against the heavy gold setting. As she stared at the strange colors, tears came to her eyes.

"Garnet is January's birthstone," she whispered. "And your birthday is next week. I'd love to wear it *as* an engagement ring, Gar," she whispered, sliding her finger into the ring. "It's perfect because it will remind me constantly of you."

Gar leaned forward and kissed her, his lips warm with promise. "It's not the usual thing," he warned. "We could get you a diamond if you like, or some emeralds to go with your beautiful eyes. I just wanted you to have this ring tonight because today is a huge step forward for us." One finger caressed her cheek lovingly.

But Beth shook her head, holding her hand out to the firelight. "This ring is absolutely perfect," she whispered, tipping her head back to stare at him. "It's exactly like you, unusual. And I love the history behind it. A diamond engagement ring is common, but this one reminds me that though we had to wait, God is always faithful. Thank you.'' She kissed him back.

''You're welcome.'' He grinned, watching her twist her hand to catch the light. ''They almost named me for that stone, you know. Thankfully, my mother thought Garnet was too effeminate a name for her son.'' Gar made a face and then patted the floor, shifting so there was room for her to sit beside him on the rug in front of the fire.

''Can you possibly be ready by Valentine's Day?'' he asked quietly. ''I know it's only a little over two weeks, but I don't want to wait anymore, and since it's so close, the day for lovers seems the perfect time to get married.''

''A Valentine's wedding would be nice,'' Beth agreed hesitantly. ''But I'd rather pick a different weekend.''

''Why?'' He seemed startled. ''Valentine's Day is supposed to be all about love.''

''I know. But it seems…well, trite. And besides, that's my busiest day. I'd rather not be racing around doing both things at once. What about the week after?''

Gar frowned, and Beth steeled herself for what she knew was coming. His disappointed look said it all. But she had to make her feelings clear.

''Beth, you don't have to worry about the store now. I make more than enough money for both of us. We can afford to let business slide for one weekend.'' His eyes begged her to reconsider.

But Beth frowned, then shook her head. "The Enchanted Florist isn't just some hobby I want to play at, Gar. This is what I do, it's part of who I am. And I'm not going to stop doing it after we're married." She prayed he knew that much about her. "I love working with flowers. It fulfills a part of me that needs expression. I put together the idea for the Enchanted Florist at the lowest point in my life. I believed in myself and worked hard to make that dream come to fruition. I intend to see it through."

She saw an angry look pass over his face, though Gar did his best to hide it. He fiddled with his hands for a moment, then wrapped one around hers, enclosing the ring and her hand inside his fist. To Beth it was akin to losing herself in him. She felt embarrassed by that, irritated that she could even think that about the man she loved.

She thrust the traitorous idea away and concentrated on what he was saying.

"I wasn't suggesting that you forget about the store, Beth. I just thought we could take a little time for us, to celebrate our marriage. If you want, I guess we could get a justice of the peace and fit the ceremony in between orders."

"Gar!" Beth felt the tears well in her eyes. "I don't want that at all." She dashed the tears away with her hand. She wasn't a child anymore. Surely she could articulate her feelings. If she could ever figure them out.

"I never really thought about this before, but—" she gulped nervously, searching for some control "—maybe what we both need is some time to reacquaint ourselves. Ten years is a long time to be apart. People change.''

''I haven't changed.'' His lip took a stubborn downward tilt. ''I'm still in love with you. And it's been eleven years, not ten. That's a long engagement, even for us!''

''I love you, Gar. More than I even thought I did before.'' Beth curled her fingers into his, and nudged her shoulder against his. ''But you have changed. And so have I. I've changed from that person you knew back then. I grew up, learned some things. And I don't want to go back to being that scared little girl who depended completely on you for her happiness.''

''I liked that girl.'' He said it grudgingly, his eyes downcast, avoiding hers.

''I didn't. You don't want a child for a wife, Gar. You want a woman who isn't afraid to move into the future. You have your business—you're good at it, too. Why is it wrong for me to love working with flowers?''

''It's not wrong,'' he huffed, kicking the fire grate. ''It just interferes with things.''

''With what, exactly?''

''With what I'd planned, what I thought you wanted. I hoped we'd be able to get married, have a honeymoon, start our life together soon. We've waited a long time already.'' His disconsolate-looking face made her smile. ''You don't have to prove anything to me, Beth. I already know you're more than capable of doing anything you set your mind to.''

"Thank you." Beth reached up and cupped his cheek in her hand, turning his head so he faced her. She chose her words with care. "Darling, we're going to be married. I'm not letting you go. But when we're married, I want to be fully awake and aware. I intend to enjoy every moment. I don't want to be half dead from the rush of Valentine's Day when I focus all my attention on you, Mr. Winthrop."

He pulled her into his arms and kissed her breathless. "Do you realize we've completely reversed roles? I used to be the rational one, the guy who thought through every move. Now, for the first time in my life, I'd like to be impetuous, and you're the voice of reason."

"Eerie, isn't it?" She giggled. "I'd better go home," she murmured ten minutes later. "I want to talk to Ronnie, tell her about us and Dad." She got to her feet and looked around the dimly lit room for her coat. When Gar didn't rise, she glanced down and saw the frown on his face. "What?"

"You *are* going to marry me, aren't you? You're not just saying that, putting me off?" Uncertainty formed a tiny furrow in his forehead, and his dark eyes swirled with unspoken emotion.

Touched by the worry in his voice, Beth pulled open her purse and snatched out her calendar. "I'm not letting you off that easily, buster," she teased, trying to lighten the atmosphere. "Valentine's Day is on a Sunday this year. I'll marry you two weeks later. That's still in the 'love' month." She raised her eyebrows and rolled her eyes as she drawled "love". "How does that suit you, Garrett Winthrop?"

"It's a little too long, actually," he murmured as he rose and kissed her once more. "More than a month away. How will I survive?"

"You'll manage," she assured him smugly. "Come on, Gar. We've got a lot of things to discuss on the way home."

"Like what?" He pressed the screen in front of the fire a little more securely, pulled on his jacket and switched out lights as she walked outside. "All I have to do is get my tux cleaned."

"Uh-uh. I don't think so!" Beth shook her head, climbed into his car and did up her seat belt, her mind racing. "Who's going to stand up with you? And what time should we have the service? What colors do you like? And how many guests should we invite?"

Gar stared at her quizzically for several moments, then came back to reality as he slammed her door shut, rounded the hood and climbed into his own seat. He pressed the key into the ignition and backed out of the drive. "Did I mention that I like the idea of eloping?"

"Don't even think about it," she warned. Then her face brightened. "I've got to find a dress. A real wedding dress." She mused on that for a good part of the way back before noticing his silence. "Is something wrong?"

"You never said if you liked the house. Not that you have to. We can sell it if you don't. Build something else maybe?"

Beth smiled.

"It's a lovely house," she murmured quietly. "And I love all that cedar. You did a wonderful job."

"But?"

"Why do you say that?" She blinked innocently.

"I can tell there's something you aren't saying," he told her with a smart-aleck grin. "You haven't changed that much, no matter what you say, Beth Ainslow. Spill it."

"It's just that I'm not sure if I can live this far out of town. Right now the store is just a few minutes from Wintergreen, and I can run back to it after dinner if I have to do the books or finish something. But this drive seems more like twenty minutes."

"Thirty, if you don't speed." He stared straight ahead. "I was hoping we'd have some time to ourselves."

"We will," she assured him. "Lots of it, I promise. But I'll still be in charge of Ronnie, and I have to think about the future. Don't forget about her."

"I have not forgotten about anything," he mumbled, face gloomy as he focused on the road. "I just hope you don't."

Beth pretended she hadn't heard the cranky note in his voice. They would both have to make adjustments. But they could do that. Couldn't they?

"Why so glum, chum?" Jordan Andrews slapped Gar on the back before flopping down beside him on Beth's old sofa. "This is your engagement party.

You're supposed to be ecstatic, aren't you? Or did I get that part wrong?''

"I am ecstatic," Gar muttered as he stared into the ruby gleam of his punch. "Completely and totally ecstatic. Deliriously enraptured."

"Could have fooled me. You look like your dog just died." Jordan took the glass away and set it on the table. "What's the matter?"

"To answer your questions in order, I don't have a dog, everything, and nothing."

"Well, that's about as clear as this sludgy hot chocolate. Care to elaborate?"

Gar knew Jordan. He knew the other man would no more leave this subject alone than a hungry dog would leave a big, juicy bone. Jordan might be a computer nerd of the highest order, but he always tried to make everyone as happy as himself. It was an annoying trait that merely emphasized the differences between them.

"I don't really want to tell all, thanks. It just has been a little hectic lately. I feel like I never get five seconds with Beth, and when I do, somebody decides we need a party with half the town invited." He saw the red flush on Jordan's cheekbones and sighed, wishing he'd taped his beak closed. "Sorry, pal. I know you and Caitlin meant well. You did invite everyone, didn't you?"

Jordan nodded. "Yup! Everyone we could think of. We thought you and Beth deserved a party to celebrate. It's been quite a week, hasn't it? You guys finally get engaged, the youth center gets under way, Beth moves to her new store, and your dad announces his plans. Sorry if we ruined your evening."

"Nah, forget it. I'm just tired, I guess." Gar glanced around the room at the hoards of busily chattering people, and decided he was too tired to hang around here much longer.

"I'm not surprised. That new merger your dad's working on will be a doozy for the bank, won't it?"

"Yeah, I guess." Gar decided to 'fess up. Maybe it would help. "The truth is, Jordan, I don't care much about that merger. First Federal has had some problems in the past. And they're totally averse to taking on clients they term at-risk."

"And you don't like that." Jordan nodded. "That's easy to understand. Your grandfather didn't operate on the same principles. But it's a whole new world, Garrett. What went on then, what was perfectly acceptable to Gramps in his day, simply isn't feasible today."

"And that's good?" Gar glared at him, disgruntled to think that someone else was against his ideas for self-funded economic growth in Oakburn.

"I didn't say that. You are in a bad mood!" Jordan's head lifted as Beth's joyful laugh rang around the room. "At least someone is enjoying herself. Now, back to the point. Which is? What's at the root of your unease, Gar?"

"Tyler." It wasn't easy to admit, and Garrett wasn't ready to spill everything. But lately Ty's actions had been bothering him. "I don't know what's up with that kid lately. I've been covering for him for months. His grades are down, he's dropped all athletics, he isn't on the debate club anymore, and I almost have to carry him physically into the bank.''

''So, the boy's going through a phase. Leave him alone and he'll grow out of it.'' Jordan took several sweets off the platter his wife passed before him and popped one into his mouth. ''He's a kid, he's supposed to explore things.''

''He can't afford to fool around too long, though. If he doesn't do something about those math marks, he's going to be attending summer school. And I assure you that my father will come down hard on him then.'' Gar shook his head at Caitlin's offer, smiled at her, then leaned back. ''Lately all he wants to do is hang around with Ronnie.''

''So? What's wrong with that?'' Jordan sniffed. ''Nobody's more college-oriented than that girl. She'll steer him right.''

''I'm not so sure of that. I don't like to talk about this with Beth, but I think the two of them are spending too much time together. They're always out riding. Or else they disappear for hours, and when you ask, they say they were talking.'' He snorted in disbelief. ''What in the world do they have to talk about? They're with each other almost every moment of the day as it is now. There's no time for anything new to have happened!''

''Ah, young love.'' Jordan wiggled his eyebrows and made calf eyes. ''What's the matter? Don't you remember what being a teenager is like?''

Gar frowned, reliving the scene he'd inadvertently glimpsed yesterday. ''That's just what has me worried. I don't think they're the least bit in love. More like best buds, pals.''

Jordan shook his head, his eyes glinting with laughter. "You need to have a frank talk with someone, Gar. Refresh your memory.''

"No, I'm serious." He hesitated, then relaxed. "Today I went looking for them when Dad was about ready to throw a hissy fit. Ty's supposed to work at the bank Friday afternoons, but he never showed. I went out to Fairwinds, and sure enough, he was there, with Ronnie, sitting on a fence on the river property by the Sullivans. They were talking a mile a minute.''

"About…?'' Jordan prodded.

"I didn't catch all of it. She told him he had to go with what he thought was right, that he couldn't allow me or Dad or anyone else to sway him. When they spotted me, they both hushed up. I felt like a fifth wheel.''

"As you were supposed to. Nobody likes to be spied on." Jordan held up a hand as Gar began to protest. "I know, you weren't spying, but it may have looked like that to them. What did Beth say about it all?''

"Like I had time to discuss it with her!" Gar heaved himself to his feet. "The only thing I know is that we're getting married on the last day of February. The rest of our wedding is a mystery. We had more communication when she lived up north." At Jordan's raised eyebrows, Gar flushed and shook his head.

"Sorry. But part of that is true. Beth is run off

her feet with this Sweetheart Banquet thing. And Valentine's Day. And maybe even the wedding, for all I know. There's no time to just relax with each other, to talk."

"So help her out."

"Huh?" Gar wondered if he was losing his hearing. Surely he was a little young for that. Or maybe it was his mind. How early did the little gray cells start keeling over?

He glanced at Jordan, but his friend certainly didn't look bothered in the least by his age. In fact, he was even now ogling a tray of chocolate-covered almonds.

"Tell her you'll take over the wedding. All she has to do is get herself a dress. You look after the rest. You tell her the details, of course. If she objects, you change them. If she doesn't, she lives with it." Jordan shrugged, intimating that the outrageous idea made perfect sense to him.

"You might also bribe Ronnie into helping out at the store more and riding less. Try clothes. Girls always like more clothes. My sisters taught me that early." He shoved his glasses farther up his nose. "It's just an idea, of course."

"And a good one." Gar rubbed his hands together in glee, his brain busy. "I know two grumpy old men who would just love to help out with this wedding. And getting Dad out of the office would give me some freedom in these negotiations." He struggled up from the sofa, freeing himself only after an intense battle with the overwhelming cushions.

"Don't leave me here."

Gar grinned and held out a hand to Jordan. "I'll get you out on one condition, pal."

Jordan stayed where he was, his golden eyes suspicious. "What's the condition?"

"You help me out with the wedding without any interference from your wife. Is it a deal?"

"Is what a deal? What are you two up to now?" Clay Matthews's voice seemed loud to Gar.

"Keep it down, will you? And if you make the same promise, I'll let you in on our little secret."

Clay nodded, his face full of curiosity. "Okay, but can we get Jordan out of that thing? I think he's going to hyperventilate if he folds up like that for much longer."

Gar heaved the big man out of the sofa and waited a moment while he caught his breath.

"You two are to meet me tomorrow morning at 9:00 a.m. at the bank. We have a lot to talk about."

"But it's Saturday," Clay protested. "I like to sleep in on Saturday. Besides, the bank's closed."

"Exactly." Gar grinned at both of them. "Be there." He put his glass down on the table, slapped a hand on each man's shoulder and smiled. "As much as I thank you for this party, Jordan, I'm going to collect Beth. There's something we need to discuss."

Then he turned and prepared to thread his way through the mob of well-wishers that surrounded the tiny blonde he loved more than life. As he went, Gar heard Clay's confused question.

"What's so important the guy has to leave in the middle of his own party?"

Jordan's answer was low-voiced, almost secretive. "Be at the café at eight-thirty and I'll tell you. But for Pete's sake, don't tell Maryann where you're going. No women."

Gar smiled as he pressed past the mayor, two members of the youth center committee and a woman who'd been dealing for eons with his family's bank.

"Excuse me, folks," he said loudly. "I need to steal this beautiful woman away from you for a while."

Amid the catcalls and silly, mocking remarks, he bundled Beth into her jacket, shoved her gloves into her hand and propelled her out the door, stopping just long enough to grab his own coat.

"Garrett Winthrop! What in the world are you up to?"

He ignored the plaintive sound of her voice and ushered her outside, his hand firmly planted on her back.

"What are you doing? Our guests—"

"Can wait. I need to discuss something with you."

"Really?" Her green eyes glowed in the streetlight. "What's so important that it couldn't wait until after the party?"

"Our wedding."

She groaned. "Gar, you know how busy I've been. I just haven't had time to do anything yet."

"I know." He smiled to show he wasn't upset,

linked her arm in his and set off at a brisk pace toward the park. "Beth, my love, I'd like to propose something."

"Again?" She grinned up at him, her eyes sparkling. "I thought we did that already."

"Be quiet, woman. I'm serious." And in the dark snowy night, with the lights and laughter of Wintergreen behind them, Garrett explained his idea, adding new twists as he went.

"Well? What do you think?" He waited breathlessly for her response, praying she wouldn't turn him down.

"I say, I'm marrying the smartest man east of the Pacific Ocean. As well as the brashest, the nerviest, the sweetest, most thoughtful fellow God could have given me. And I'm taking you up on it, all of it. Just remember two weeks from now, when you're buried under To-Do lists, that you *offered.*"

"Oh, I'll remember. Just make sure *you* do when I pick the wrong color."

"Colors don't matter to me." She laughed at the very idea. Seconds later a frown replaced that smile. "Unless it's black. I don't want a black wedding."

"Trust me," he encouraged as Beth's arms wrapped around his waist and she hugged him close. Garrett smiled to himself.

*All right, Lord,* he prayed silently. *One problem down, one to go. Why don't I feel Ty will be as easy to handle?*

Gar fancied he heard a light burble of laughter drop down from heaven along with the fluffy snowflake that landed on his nose. But it must have been his imagination for when he looked up, cold, wet snow got caught in his lashes and he couldn't see a thing, let alone hear any voices.

I can do it, he told himself confidently. No problem.

There was that laughter again. Must be someone else in the park.

# *Chapter Ten*

~❧~

"They did what?"

A week later Beth sighed, rubbed her fist against her temple and counted to ten, fifteen, no, twenty. She glared at the speaker phone malevolently as she pulled her finger free of a rose thorn.

"They went to Minneapolis, Gar. To see an exhibit. They went with the youth group."

"Oh, yeah." A long pause. "I thought that was for a rock concert. That 'cool' singer, what's his name?" His voice echoed back, full of confusion.

"Denise D'Angelo is *her* name. And yes, they went for that. But when she phoned, Ronnie said they saw the ad while they were there and decided to go to an exhibit." She stared at the layers of greenery that waited to be formed into table edging, and felt tiredness swamp her.

"My brother went to an *art* exhibit? Willingly?" The disbelief was obvious.

"Gar, I'm up to my neck in plans for this over-done banquet that my dear, sweet friends came up with. Believe me, I would not choose this moment to play a joke on you." She swallowed a mouthful of cold, stale coffee, and made a face. "Anyway, what's so bad about Ty going to an exhibit? We can all do with exposure to the finer things in life."

"But an art exhibit?—" he huffed "—Unreal."

Beth frowned. "Ronnie didn't actually say 'art.' I don't think," she mused. "I guess I just assumed that part. What other kind of exhibit is there?"

"You're asking me? I haven't a clue. And when it comes to Ty, I would have said it would be either food or horses. What was wrong with coming home with the rest of the group?"

"I don't know." Beth puffed, blowing cool air onto her forehead. "I don't know any more than I've told you."

"Kids! If they'd only think first."

"You're wasting time, Gar. Of course, I would have preferred that they got on the bus with the rest of the group, but it's too late to say that now. They missed it, and someone has to go get them."

A long, drawn-out silence greeted her words. Then a sigh.

"You're not asking me to go, are you? Because I can't. Not now. I'm in the middle of sorting through Dad's latest brain wave."

Garrett's tone was less than cordial. In fact, he sounded harassed, as if he'd been hit with one too many things in the past hour.

Beth knew exactly how he felt. Three funerals of

prominent citizens, an impromptu wedding and then this banquet with all of Caitlin's changes and Mary-ann's add-ons. Not that she resented the business or the income. No, she was thrilled with both. But how would she ever get everything ready?

"Then when? I don't suppose it would hurt them to stay overnight, though according to Ronnie, nei-ther one of them has enough for a hotel room." She tried to think of another idea, but lately all she saw was more and more work.

"Can't you go?" The request hinted that it was her turn. "After all, I've been doing all this planning and stuff for the wedding."

"Along with our fathers." She nodded. "I heard. And for your information, I've been working, too, you know. You act as though I have nothing to do but wait for your phone calls!" Beth heard the words as if they came from someone else's mouth, and shame filled her. "I'm sorry, Gar," she apolo-gized. "I'm just very tired. Okay, if you can't, you can't. I'll have to drop what I'm doing and go."

She stared at the mess that lay around the work-room, remnants of a Saturday that should have been finished two hours ago. Everyone else had left at six, but she'd stayed on, determined to make a dent in the Valentine preparations that were now only a week away. Boxes of expensive Belgian chocolates sat in the cooler, waiting for her to get the showcase ready. If it didn't happen soon, she would lose a lot of money.

"I can leave in about fifteen minutes if I hustle."

Silence. Then a rustle of paper came through the phone.

"I'll go with you," Gar announced. "I need a break, and I need to see you. That's more important than work. We can go over wedding things on the drive. How's that sound?"

Beth's heart lifted. "Actually, it sounds wonderful. I've barely seen you this week. And I don't think we've had more than a three-minute conversation since that party last week."

"It's that crazy youth center. They keep changing their minds. I knew it was a mistake to let Jordan talk me into sitting on that board. Carpet, no carpet, pop machine or food booth, CDs or cassettes. The list goes on and on."

Beth straightened. "Jordan talked you into that? I thought you were asked as part of your council duties..." She let the words trail away, shook her head and refocused. "Never mind. I don't care how you got on it. All I want to do is see the thing opened. Why did they have to choose February for that?"

Gar laughed and the sound was music to her ears. She'd missed him.

"Guess they figured it would be a quiet month. Shows what they know." He cleared his throat. "We're wasting time, Beth. I'll pick you up in ten minutes. Okay?"

Fifteen minutes later, accompanied by chips and sodas, she leaned back against the car's leather upholstery and breathed a sigh of relief.

"It feels good to sit down for a while," she mumbled, resting her head on the back of her seat. "My legs are so tired!"

"I feel like I've been sitting for days." Gar shifted uncomfortably.

"The negotiations?" When he nodded, she smiled sympathetically. "How's it going?"

"It's not. We're at an impasse. Dad's not too happy with me right now, but I'm not going to go along with something I don't feel is good for Oakburn."

"What do they want to do?" she asked curiously. She flicked open a can and placed it in the cup holder.

"Call in a few loans for starters. From people who can't afford to pay them right now. Thanks." He took a drink and replaced the can.

"It's a good thing you borrowed your dad's car. We'd never squeeze the kids into yours." Beth opened her own drink and then offered him a package of chips. "Is the bank overextended or something?"

He shook his head. "Not at all. We're well covered. Sure, we've got a few bad debts that we will probably never recover—who hasn't? Still, all in all, I think we're in pretty good shape. It's just that these guys want to make it as much of a sure thing as possible."

"I guess we'd all like to know that we weren't taking any risks. But if we don't, nothing much gets accomplished in life. Ronnie and I were talking about this the other day. She thinks she should find a college nearer Oakburn, just in case I need her.'' She smiled, remembering her sister's generous offer.

''What about me? Don't forget, we'll be married.'' He looked offended by the very idea, and Beth forced down a smile.

''I'm not forgetting, neither is she. I think she feels that I'll need her moral support.''

''For what?'' Gar's disgruntled voice was barely held in check. ''I'm not an ogre.''

''Close,'' Beth teased, her head tilted to one side as she studied his profile. ''You do furrow your brow something fierce when anyone dares question you.'' She laughed out loud at his frown. ''But really, I think she's more worried about me standing up against your father. Ronnie thinks I'm a wimp.''

''She doesn't know you very well, then. Even I know better than that.'' Free of the town, Gar set the cruise control and leaned back to relax. ''You've always gone after exactly what you wanted.''

''Not always. And never with your family. I let all the gloss and hype that surrounds your dad overwhelm me. Don't worry,'' she hastened to add, ''I'm not going to do it again. But I do have to guard against taking the easy way out.''

''That's what I've been doing with Ty. I know how overbearing Dad can get, and I always try to shield him. But he's got to learn to face responsibility. Tonight is just another example of his immaturity. It's time he grew up.''

''He's a teenager, Garrett. They're supposed to be irresponsible once in a while.'' Beth rushed to the kids' defense, unable to understand Gar's anger.

"That's a good excuse, isn't it? 'Poor little kid, let's let him ride on someone else's coattails for a while.' No way! I took my duties seriously when I was his age."

"Maybe a little too seriously." The words slipped out. Obviously, tiredness loosened her tongue.

"What does that mean?" His dark eyes veered from the road just long enough to glare at her. "Are we going back to blaming each other?"

"No, of course not! It's just…" How could she explain what she meant?

"Just what?" His tone told her it would be better if she stopped now.

But she couldn't. The questions lay there, waiting to surface. Wasn't it better to deal with her doubts now, before things got blown out of proportion?

"I've often wondered this, Gar. Tonight I'm going to ask it." Beth took a deep breath and plunged in. "What would you have done if you hadn't known you were expected to follow in your father's footsteps?"

The silence that stretched between them told its own story. Taut with strain, full of things unsaid, it hung there.

"I've always known I would be at the bank," he muttered at last. "It's a part of who I am, of what I was brought up with. And if you think I resent that, you're wrong. I like banking. I like the challenge of finding ways to make people's dreams come true."

Beth nodded. "I know you like the numbers part of it. But the dream part, that's what you do in your own time, in your own business. It's not something that you really do much of at the bank, is it?''

Gar took another swallow of his drink, his eyes fixed on the dark ribbon of highway ahead. Occasionally he'd glance at her, but she couldn't discern his true feelings. So why did she doubt him? Why did she feel he kept hiding something about himself—some part that he never let anyone see?

''The flower shop was your dream. We filled that request.'' The words had a harsh edge to them.

''But I wasn't a good risk, and I doubt whether your father would have granted my loan without some pressure from you. Am I right?'' She waited, knowing deep inside that it was the truth.

''It doesn't matter how the dream gets filled. The fact that it does should be enough.''

''Maybe.'' She chewed on another chip, considering his words.

''But we're straying from the topic.''

''Which was?'' He sounded irritated.

''Duty. I think you would have done something completely different if your father hadn't groomed you for the bank since the day you were born.'' She held up the chip bag and waited while he found several with his free hand.

''Maybe. But I had a duty, and I did it. It didn't kill me, I make good money at it and there are times when it is very fulfilling. That's what I want for Ty.''

''And if he doesn't want to spend his life in the bank?'' She held her breath and waited as he absorbed such a rebellious thought.

"He will. He knows that's his place." Gar drove steadily on for a few minutes, then leaned over to pat her hand. "Why don't I catch you up on our wedding? It's going to be at least another hour 'til we get there."

And that's the end of it, Beth mused to herself, only half listening to his description of the guest list. He doesn't even want to consider that there could be an alternative life choice for Ty.

If we have kids, are they going to have to be involved in the bank, too? she mused to herself. Or will they have the freedom to find their own niche? She tilted her seat back more comfortably, murmured her consent to matching wedding bands, then closed her eyes. Just for a moment.

She dreamed of four towheaded boys dressed in three-piece suits, marching to the beat of an unseen drummer. Somehow she knew these were her children—hers and Gar's. But they didn't want to go to the bank. They wanted to go play in the park.

"Beth? Come on, wake up. We're almost there." Gar's hand lifted from her shoulder as he manipulated the car in and out of traffic. "What street did you say this place is on?"

"Just a minute. I wrote it down somewhere. Oh yeah, here it is." She blinked groggily.

"The corner of Fifth and Fifteenth." She straightened as the city lights flashed past. Eventually they reached the right corner. "There, that's Ronnie in her pink jacket."

Gar eased the car to the curb and pressed the automatic door locks so the two teens could tumble into the back seat.

"You guys are lifesavers," Ronnie gushed. "I just couldn't think what else to do. The bus had gone by the time we got back to the hall. Sorry, sis. I know you were up to your eyeballs in work."

"It's my fault, not hers. I had to see that display when I saw it advertised in the paper. I just didn't think it would take so long to get back." Ty fastened his seat belt and then looked at his brother's rigid back. "Thanks for coming, bro."

"'Didn't think' is right. Do you realize I was in the middle of some important negotiations? And Beth has piles of work to do, too. We can't just dump everything and run off to rescue you because you 'didn't think.'" Gar stared straight ahead, but his voice was tight with anger.

"It's okay, Gar. I'll catch up. Ronnie'll help me." Beth tried to smooth things over.

"Well, that's just lovely. Good for Ronnie. But who is going to give me a helping hand? It won't be Tyler. He hasn't got the foggiest notion of what's going on nowadays, because he hasn't been in to do his *job* in weeks."

Beth's temper started a slow simmer. "Garrett, do we have to go over this again now? They know they made a mistake. They won't do it again. Can't we just relax?"

"Relax?" He stared at her as if she had suggested he rob a bank. "You don't learn anything by relaxing and letting your standards drop."

Beth was glad the light was temporarily red, because his attention was certainly not on his driving. She closed her eyes and prayed for control of her tongue. Behind them a horn honked, and she grabbed the seat as he lurched forward, his foot heavy on the gas.

"Garrett. Slow down. I don't want to get killed on the way home." To her relief, he did lift his foot until they were through the city. "Are you two hungry?" she asked, turning to glance at the repentant pair.

"Starved," Ronnie admitted.

"Do you think we could pull in over there and pick up some burgers and fries?" Beth pointed to the drive-thru, considered the car they were in and changed her mind. "Or maybe we should go inside. We don't want to mess up your father's car."

"No, we wouldn't want to do that." The stinging mockery came from tightly clenched lips.

Beth ignored him. Once parked, she climbed out and motioned to the others. "Come on. I'm buying." Gar stayed in the car. "Aren't you coming inside?" she demanded as the others slipped and slid across the icy parking lot.

"I'll stay here, thanks."

Beth sighed. She'd disagreed with him and now he was pouting. Surely this wasn't a good omen.

"Get out of the car, Garrett Winthrop, or I'll make the biggest scene you ever hope to see." She kept the teasing out of her voice, her eyes solemn and her mouth in a straight line. "Now!"

"Sometimes, you're a royal pain," he muttered finally, easing himself out from behind the wheel.

"The feeling is mutual. They're kids, for Pete's sake. Will you cut them some slack?" Sure that he was following her, Beth walked inside the fast-food place and ordered for them all, not even bothering to consult Garrett who'd gone to find a table.

While Ronnie and Ty chatted about the concert, readily answering Beth's questions, Gar sat silently, his face gloomy. They were slurping up the last bit of their milk shakes when he finally spoke.

"So what was so great about this art exhibit that you had to go across town to see?" His long lean fingers picked up a French fry, inspected it and then placed it in his mouth as his eyes pinned them down.

"Oh, it wasn't an art exhibit." Ronnie grinned, her eyes dancing. "It was an exhibit by a group of international chefs. You should have seen the stuff they made. Ty's eyes were this big." She made a circular motion with her fingers. "He's going to try a couple of the recipes out next week."

"Chefs?" Beth repeated.

"You went to look at food?" Gar sounded shocked. "Why in the world would you do that?"

"'Cause Ty's gonna be a world-famous chef someday. You should taste his caramel banana torte!" She rolled her eyes, head lolling back. "It's to die for. Ow! Why'd you kick me, Ty?"

"Cooking is a good hobby to have," Beth offered, smiling at the red-faced boy who now shifted uneasily in his seat. "You can come and practise on us anytime. Especially if you're making cookies. Ronnie's are disgusting!"

"Oh, it's not a hobby," Ronnie burst in, her eyes

glittering with excitement. "Ty wants to train as a chef. He's even found the best school."

"What?" Gar's voice roared above the crowded room, causing patrons to turn and frown at him. "You want to be a cook? A *cook!*"

He made the vocation sound as if it were a fate worse than death, Beth fumed silently. She saw Ty focus his eyes on his lap, his hands twisting beneath the edge of the table. His cheeks burned a bright, embarrassed red. When he finally glanced up, she saw the defiance in the depths of those usually laughing eyes.

"Yes, a cook. A chef. That's what I want."

"Well, you can forget it right now. I suppose it's okay as a hobby, but it's not something you do for the rest of your life. Get a mitt and get in the game, kid. We're talking about a career."

"There are some very good careers for chefs." Tyler's voice was soft but steady. Clearly, though he hadn't expected to discuss it tonight, like this, he'd done some preparation. "And they work in fascinating places. Someday I'm going to open my own restaurant. I'm going to train in Europe."

Beth silently applauded the smooth controlled tone, though she knew the boy was hurt by his brother's scoffing.

"Don't be a fool. What do you know about cooking?" Gar's voice raked out scathingly. "Nothing. You've never done it. And I'm sure it doesn't begin to pay well. It takes years for these men to make it to the top."

"I've been working in the kitchen for months,

Gar. Those things you took to Ronnie's dad at the potluck, I made those. And I don't care about the money," Ty added.

"Of course you don't. You've never really had to earn any, have you?" Gar shook his head, completely disregarding Ty's answers. "I don't understand any of this."

"I don't think we need to discuss it right now. Are you two finished?" Beth gathered up the soiled papers and cardboard containers as she waited. "Want some dessert?"

"No, thanks."

They both looked glum, deflated, as if they'd lost their oomph. It hurt her to see Ty's disillusionment with the brother he'd trailed after since he'd learned to walk. She'd have to talk to Garrett, make him understand. Somehow.

"Okay, let's get on the road, then. You two can snooze for a while. Gar, do you want me to drive?" She stood, holding the tray as she stared into his eyes.

"Believe me, I'm wide awake now." The scathing response made her bristle.

"Fine. Let's go." She slipped the car keys out of Gar's hand and tossed them at Ty. "You two go ahead. We'll be there in a minute."

"Don't start with me, Beth. I'm furious. This is why the kid's been avoiding work. He's been playing at cooking."

"What's wrong with that? Other than the fact that it isn't *your* choice?" She stood directly in front of him, daring him to answer.

"Ty's future is with the bank. There's security, a good income. Everything's all set up."

"And he doesn't want it. So now what?"

Gar stood, easing her out of the way as he flexed his shoulders tiredly. "I don't know. He'll have to give up this silly notion, of course. Dad will have a heart attack."

"Well, then he'll have a heart attack. Hopefully he'll get over it." Beth smiled to soften her words. "Gar, Tyler can't live his life the way you or your father want. It's his life. He only gets one chance at it and he has to make the best of that. Let him do it his own way."

"Don't be foolish."

She smiled sadly. "Foolish? I don't think so. I know exactly how Ty feels. I had a dream once. I wanted it so badly, I could almost taste it. I put my heart and mind and soul into learning everything I could to make that dream come true. And eventually, when I opened the Enchanted Florist, it did."

She peered at him quizzically. "Haven't you ever wanted something so badly that you were willing to do whatever it took to make it reality, Garrett?"

He sat there, silent but brooding, filled with anger, his mouth taut.

"Yes," he enunciated finally. "I have. But I didn't get it. And I managed to survive."

"I see." She tapped her finger on the table. "You get so much joy and pleasure out of your father's bank that you now want Ty to ignore whatever hopes and dreams he has because you're positive he'll find his true calling there, too. Am I right?"

"He's too young to know——" Gar began.

"But that's exactly the same mistake your father made about us!" She couldn't believe they were doing this again. Hadn't they learned anything? "He thought you were too young, I wasn't good enough, we needed to grow up. And he was *wrong*."

Garrett stared at her in astonishment, his mouth open.

"Don't you see, Gar? This is always at the root of our disagreements. Now it's a barrier between you and your brother. You want both Tyler and me to give up what we've chosen for ourselves, what we really enjoy."

She swallowed, searching for the right words. "It's not right to do that to anyone, Gar. I wouldn't ask you to give up the bank. Not ever. I know how much pleasing your father and helping the people in Oakburn means to you. You wouldn't be the same person, the man that I love, if you didn't put every effort into helping people get what they want out of life."

He gave a wry smile. "That's my job, ma'am. I'm a financial advisor. I help people achieve their dreams."

She nodded. "I know that. And I think it's wonderful work. But what else do you want from life?"

"I don't know what you mean. The bank takes up all my time now." He looked mystified.

"Exactly! And that isn't good."

"It's not?" He adjusted the ketchup bottle, moving it first to the left, then to the right. "Why?"

Beth took a deep breath and plunged in. "What

would you do if everyone in Oakburn was on the road to achieving what they wanted from life—their dream? What would you do next?''

''Do?'' He frowned. ''Look for new clients.''

''There aren't any more clients, the bank is doing fine, your father is happy, your life is on a roll. Now, what do you want?''

His eyes clouded in puzzlement. ''I don't know.''

''But don't you have a whole list of things you'd like to try someday, if you have the chance?''

''What kind of things?'' He looked nonplussed. ''You mean hobbies?'' He gave the word a distinctly horrible sound.

''Not necessarily. Just things you want to do.'' Seeing that she was getting nowhere, Beth decided to help him out. ''For instance, I've always wanted to ride in a hot air balloon. Or go to Hawaii.''

''I've already been there, but we could go again.'' He looked pleased by the thought.

Beth sighed tiredly, wondering if she'd been wrong to even bring up this subject. But it worried her. Was he so driven by his father's idea of success that he had no ambitions that were totally his own?

''Isn't there anything that really thrills you?'' she finally demanded. ''Anything that you'd like to try, just once, to see if it's all it's cracked up to be?''

A faraway look came into those rich gray eyes, and Beth could almost see the wheels in his mind turning.

''Okay, you've thought of something. I can see it as plainly as the nose on your face. What is it?'' She waited, breath suspended.

"You'll think it's silly," he stalled, pretending to fiddle with his collar.

Beth reached out and placed a hand on his arm. When he looked up, she met his embarrassed gaze and smiled steadily. "I won't think it's silly," she promised. "Tell me."

His eyes assessed her seriousness. Eventually he nodded, apparently satisfied that she could be told.

"I'd like to go sky diving," he muttered at last.

"Sky diving?" She gulped.

Garrett, the man who never took a risk without thinking everything out logically and carefully, wanted to throw himself out of an airplane at six-thousand feet with nothing but a dinky piece of silk to depend on?

"I knew you'd think it was juvenile." He picked up his gloves, pulled them on, and then, finger by finger, removed them. "I do, too. My father would never allow it."

Indignation surged to the fore. "Never allow it?" She gathered her belongings, squashed the empty containers into a garbage can and pulled her purse over one shoulder. Then she turned her attention back to him. "You're twenty-nine years old, Garrett. Don't you think it's time you decided whose life you're living? As for me, I've got to get some sleep. Valentine's Day is only one week away. Let's go."

The ride home was not restful. Silence, filled with foreboding, stretched among them. Several times Beth heard Ronnie and Ty whispering. But she ignored them.

Instead, Beth focused on what needed to be done

for the banquet that had gotten out of control. By the time Gar pulled up in front of Wintergreen, she was more than ready for sleep. She leaned over to kiss his cheek.

"Think about what I said, Gar. Everybody has to make their own mistakes. Even Ty. Good night to you both. Ronnie?"

In a calm, dignified manner, she made her escape, while he sat puzzling over her words. She shooed Ty back into the car, kept Ronnie behind her and closed the door firmly on both of the Winthrops.

"Let him chew on that for a while," she muttered as she climbed the stairs to bed, more exhausted than she'd been in months.

# Chapter Eleven

"I hate this Sweetheart's Ball. How did it get to be a ball anyway? This started out as a banquet." Beth grumbled and complained as she rearranged the red and white carnations in their vases for the fifth time that afternoon. "And if you move these one more time, Caitlin Andrews, I'll pinch your fingers!"

Caitlin chuckled, her eyes dancing. "A little moody, aren't we?" she teased. "For a girl who just got engaged, who's getting married in two weeks to the most handsome Garrett Winthrop, you're just the teensiest bit cranky, my dear."

"Nerves I guess. I want everything to go smoothly so I can get working on my wedding plans." Beth sighed. "I haven't even chosen a dress yet. Why can't the men be here helping? It's Saturday, all three of them are free and yet here we are, decorating for this ill-conceived banquet tonight!"

"It was not ill-conceived." Maryann sniffed. "I think it's a wonderful way to spend a Saturday night, and especially here at Fairwinds. It's so romantic!"

Beth groaned as her friend's eyes grew hazy and her hands forgot that they were supposed to be twisting a streamer. "Romantic? We'll be lucky to stagger in here after doing all this work." She began spreading rose petals down the center of each table as Maryann had requested. "They could have been hanging those things, instead of asking you to go up a ladder."

"Not this morning they couldn't." Maryann giggled. "This is the only morning they could get a plane. I never thought Clay could look so green."

A premonition, dark and suffocating, rose in Beth's stomach.

"A plane? What do they need a plane for?" she asked, carefully dropping one petal at a time as her heart sank to her toes.

Caitlin frowned at Maryann. Obviously her friend had spilled the beans. "They wouldn't say," Caitlin admitted. "But I think they're going to get something for tonight. Jordan said you'd be thrilled."

"Oh, no! Oh, please, no." She dropped the basket of petals on the floor, grabbed her coat and headed for the stairs. "You guys finish up. I'll be back later."

"Beth, where are you going?" Caitlin's voice followed her up the steps.

"To stop something before someone gets himself killed." Beth muttered the words to herself as she slammed her delivery van into reverse and took off for the municipal airport.

By the time she had arrived at the air field, parked the van and rushed to the fence that enclosed the landing strips, she'd gone over every word she could remember of Gar's—the predominant one being sky*diving*.

"He wouldn't do it," she told herself firmly, scanning the sky, which looked wintry dark and ominous. "He'd never do something so foolhardy. I'm wasting my time out here."

The low drone of an airplane engine carried on the wind, and Beth searched anxiously, expecting to see a human form come hurtling through the air toward her. Something did fall, and for a moment her heart stopped. But then she realized that it was a flurry of small papers, and they were being tossed and turned in the wind.

It wasn't Gar.

Relieved and feeling somewhat foolish, Beth returned to the van to collect her scattered thoughts. This silly panicking was doing no one any good. And she had far too much to do.

Lips tightly pursed, she drove back to the shop to help Ronnie and her assistant, Melinda, deal with the influx of customers.

"Yes, we do have delivery tomorrow. I know it's Sunday but my sister wanted to be sure people had the option if they wanted it. Sure, where do you live?" Ronnie shoved the phone between her neck and her shoulder and busily scribbled down an address.

"We'll have it there. Thanks for calling."

"Looks like you two have been running." Beth took off her coat and hung it up, eyes widening at the number of orders hanging on the To-Do peg. "Really busy?"

"Yep, you could say that." Ronnie blew her bangs off her forehead and stepped from behind the counter. "I have to help Mr. Peterson decide on something for his wife. He's been here about an hour. Can you do the phone?"

Beth nodded and picked up the receiver. "Enchanted Florist."

Between phone calls, special orders and time spent on arrangements, Beth was kept busy for the rest of the morning. She wasn't worried about returning to Fairwinds until late afternoon, when she would put the finishing touches on everything. For now, it was important to concentrate on every customer that she could.

"Hi." Garrett stood grinning in front of her worktable, his cheeks red from the cold. "Pretty busy, I see."

"Drowning." She smiled back and reached for another vase. "But I love it." She arranged the tiny pink rosebuds with fern, added some baby's breath and a ribbon, and admired her work.

"Have you got time for lunch? There is something I need to discuss about the wedding."

"Now?" She shook her head, paper-clipped the form onto the card and pushed the pick into the vase. In one fluid motion she set it in the cooler, while her other hand automatically reached for the next order.

"It's kind of important," he murmured, watching her hands fly. "I, uh, probably should have told you before this."

"Can't we discuss it here? It is my busiest day, Gar. I don't want to go for lunch. I'll get behind. Further behind."

He frowned, tipping back on his heels as he thought about it. "I suppose. You see, the thing is, I wanted—"

"Can I help, Dave?" Beth couldn't help interrupting. A young man stood waiting for her attention, and she had to acknowledge him. The other girls were busy elsewhere.

"I want to get some flowers. Something special."

Muttering a quick "Excuse me," Beth hurried toward the man. "Okay. What kind were you thinking of?"

Helping Dave didn't take long but there was a constant stream after him and it was some time before she remembered Garrett. She wasn't surprised to find he'd left. There was plenty to do at Fairwinds to get ready for the big event tonight.

"What did Gar want?" Ronnie asked later that afternoon, when a lull in customers allowed them to sip a cup of hot chocolate together.

"I don't know," Beth admitted. "I had to wait on a customer."

"Congratulations, Beth." Old Mrs. Arbuthnot smiled toothily, patting her purse. "You can mark me down. I'll be there for the wedding."

"Oh. Uh, that's really nice, Mrs. Arbuthnot. We'll look forward to having you there." Beth waited 'til the older woman had left, then turned to Ronnie. "Gar invited her to our wedding? But she wasn't on the list. We barely know her!"

"Maybe she's a friend of his." Ronnie turned away, dumping out the rest of her drink.

"But how would she know the time and stuff? She sounded like she had a personal invitation."

"Beats me." Ronnie wiped her hands down her green apron, fingered the logo that was printed on the pocket and scuffed her toe on the floor. She completely avoided Beth's glance.

As the door chime pealed its summons, she jerked forward. "I'll get it. You finish that. You've got a long night ahead."

That was odd. Ronnie never hurried to wait on a customer. She was always espousing the belief that people bought more if they could browse first.

Beth shook her head. No point in puzzling over it. There was too much to be done. She got up and wearily checked her stock. So far, so good. Her second year in business was proving she hadn't been wrong about the Enchanted Florist. She could do this, pull this off. She just had to focus.

"I'll take these to Fairwinds and set them up. You go home and change. Have a bubble bath. You're dog tired." Ronnie picked up the arrangement baskets and carried them to the back one by one. "I asked Ty to be here to drive me, just in case we got behind. I figured today would be a little rushed."

"Thank you, sweetie. You're a doll." Beth glanced around the empty shop with a satisfied smile. "We've done really well. But I'm going to have to pull an all-nighter after the banquet."

"No way! We were talking it over and we've all decided to put in an extra couple of hours tonight. That way, everything should be ready for tomorrow. We haven't got any sweethearts anyhow, so we don't much care about the banquet." Ronnie grinned at the other two women whom Beth had hired.

"This once I'm going to take you up on that." Beth tugged on her coat and grabbed her purse. "Thanks very much." She glanced at her watch. "Yikes! Is it six-thirty already? I'll have to hustle."

"Good thing I laid out your dress this morning, isn't it?" Ronnie preened, obviously pleased with herself. "Now get going. Gar is going to pick you up in twenty-five minutes."

Beth got.

At home she showered, blow-dried her hair and applied her makeup faster than she'd done in years. By the time Gar rang the doorbell, however, she was also satisfied that she *looked* better than she had in years. Evidently, Garrett agreed.

"Wow!" He walked around her twice, admiring the ruby gown with its side slit and pearl-encrusted bodice. "You look fantastic." He leaned over and kissed her. "I'll be the most envied man there."

"You look pretty spiffy yourself." She touched the glistening white shirt with one finger, admiring its silken sheen. "I don't think I ever saw you in a bow tie before."

"And after our wedding, you won't again," he muttered, tugging at his neck. "I hate 'em."

"Thank you, darling." She stood on tiptoe and pressed a kiss against his cheek. "I know you did it for me."

"I did something else for you, too," he muttered soberly. "I tried to tell you earlier, but you were too busy."

"Shouldn't we be going? You could tell me on the way." Beth reached for her faux fur coat and slipped her arms in while he held it up. "Ready?"

He nodded, holding the door so she could precede him. Once in the car, Gar seemed to find it hard to begin.

"You'd better tell me now, if you're so anxious to discuss something. We'll be there shortly."

"I hired a plane today," he blurted out.

"I know." She smiled, remembering her panic.

"Oh. You know and you aren't mad?"

"Why should I be mad? You didn't jump, did you?" She frowned at the thought.

"Jump?" It took a few moments for her meaning to sink in. "No! Of course not. Heights give me a headache. I hired the pilot to drop wedding invitations on the town."

Beth blinked, certain she'd misunderstood. "Pardon?"

"I did. I got sick and tired of your dad, my dad, my grandmother, my mother and every other Tom, Dick and Harry telling me not to forget someone.

So I had an invitation made up, and I distributed them all over the town. From the plane.''

She blinked.

"Oh. How many invitations?" she managed to ask.

"I'm not sure. A lot."

"Oh." She swallowed. "Uh, what else is happening with the wedding plans, Gar?"

"Why? Worried?" The grin on his face didn't ease her anxiety.

"If you want the truth, then yes." She made a face at his mocking laughter. "Are there turtledoves being released in the town square at noon? Who's catering? And where are we going for our honeymoon?" She frowned. "Or are we even having one? I should know so I can cover the store," she mumbled, avoiding his smugly superior look.

"I'm not telling you where, but I will tell you we're taking two weeks. Just you and me, without your sister or my grandmother or anyone else."

"I like your grandmother. She's been a real encouragement to me."

"Well, she's discouraging me. Every time you and I get five minutes together, she calls. And talks for hours. It's hard to compete."

He turned the corner into Fairwinds, then tossed her a glowering look. "And don't think you're going to sit in the study and chatter with Dinah tonight, either. I'm counting on us spending some time together, even if we do have to compete with a hundred or so other people."

"Dinah's going to be here?" Beth stared at him. "How come?"

"She's being escorted by your father. Apparently, according to her, he needs to get out more often."

"Oh, Gar, do you think that's a good idea? I mean, she's so sophisticated. Dad's, well, recovering." She felt her cheeks heat at the frown he cast her way.

"My grandmother likes Mervyn because of who he is," he said sternly. "She couldn't care less about his faults or problems. She just wants to be his friend. She says he makes her laugh."

Suitably reprimanded, Beth said no more. But as he escorted her inside his parents' sprawling home, and she took in the elegance of the rooms, she couldn't help wondering how her father would feel entering his enemy's home. She didn't want him to be embarrassed or feel out of place, but the truth was, he didn't have much in common with any of these people, young or old.

Neither, for that matter, did she. Except that she was going to be Gar's wife.

"Come on, let's get some punch. Dinner's in twenty minutes."

Beth soon forgot about her father amid the happy chatter and laughter of the merry group. Once they'd sat down at the elegantly appointed tables, the oldest sweethearts were announced and received a pair of tickets to a stage production in a nearby town.

Jordan Andrews was at his best as host, and he made everyone howl with laughter at his silly jokes. "We'll be having these contests all through the evening, so don't be surprised if you win something. You're all fair game.''

He proposed a toast, and everyone clinked glasses as the waiters carried out their meals and began serving.

''I don't see your parents,'' Beth murmured, leaning to one side as the waiter placed her plate in front of her. She caught a hint of Gar's aftershave, and smiled.

This felt right, good. She was a part of this; she belonged here because she belonged to Gar. The delicate china, crystal glasses and silver serving dishes didn't impress her nearly as much as they had the last time she'd been here. They were just objects.

''Today is the day my parents were married, thirty-five years ago. They flew to Paris this morning to celebrate.''

''Isn't that romantic?'' Their tablemates smiled and began chatting about true love.

But Beth didn't hear most of it. She caught a glimpse of her father seated beside Dinah Winthrop, and her breath stopped in her throat. He looked nervous, ill at ease in the poorly fitted black suit that had definitely seen better days. His plate sat before him, but he made no effort to eat anything; he fiddled with first one fork and then another.

To her credit, Dinah was smiling and obviously doing her best to make him feel comfortable. From time to time she'd lean forward, touch his arm, ask a question. Beth could see the movement of her father's lips, his answering smile—but there was still confusion in his eyes.

"Excuse me," she murmured, easing away from the table. "No, go ahead and eat, Gar. I just want a word with Dad. I'll be right back."

Garrett frowned, but he sat back down, his eyes intense. She could feel them burning into her back as she threaded her way to Dinah's table.

"Hello, Dinah, Dad. You two look stunning." She carefully placed her hand on Mervyn's shoulder, hoping to infuse a little confidence as she smiled at them both.

"So do you, dear. Absolutely lovely. You have a beautiful daughter, Mervyn." Dinah's expressive eyes thanked Beth for her help. "I persuaded your father that this was one event he couldn't miss, even if he had to escort an old woman like me. And then they gave us this table for two. Wasn't that lovely?"

Mervyn seemed to relax, just a little, as he covered Dinah's hand with his own. "I'm glad she asked me," he told Beth. "I didn't realize you'd fit in here so well. You look as if you were born to this kind of thing."

Beth couldn't stop the laugh that burbled up inside. "Looks can be deceiving, Dad. I'm still just plain old Beth, but I dress up okay." She glanced around, saw Jordan heading for the microphone and murmured, "See you later." Then she hurried back to her place.

Gar held her chair. "Your food is cold."

Because she was concentrating on his words, Beth missed whatever it was Jordan had said that made the room erupt in clapping. She turned to see her father stumble to his feet, his face beet red as he took Dinah's hand and half bowed to the assembled group. Once the old woman was seated, Mervyn ducked into his own chair, keeping his eyes down.

"Now it's time to vote for the cuddliest sweethearts," Jordan boomed. "I've already had one nomination for Maryann and Clay Matthews." The crowd burst in whistles and catcalls. "Yes, I suppose you can't expect these newlyweds to remember they're in public and not hold hands under the table, can you?"

Beth met Caitlin's grin with her own, and they both smiled as a red-faced Maryann jerked her hand out of Clay's.

"You haven't been doing too badly in that department yourself, Jordan!" someone called out. Everyone agreed, and Herman Nethers took over the microphone just long enough to demand that both pairs stand and accept the prize of chocolate kisses.

"You'll have to share, but I'm sure you two don't mind. They're not nearly as good as the real ones, anyhow." Herman laughed at his own joke long and hard, until his wife nudged him and he sat down.

"We're going to have the waiters clear the tables now. While you're doing that, prepare for a very sweet dessert."

The waiters worked fast, removing dishes and refilling wineglasses as they went. Beth frowned when she noticed that someone had given her father a glass of wine, but she relaxed a little after noticing that it hadn't been touched.

"He's fine, Beth. Dinah will look after him. Just

relax and enjoy the evening.'' Gar's hand closed over hers.

Beth grinned. ''I don't think you should do that anymore,'' she told him quietly. ''Everyone seems to be watching us already, and we don't want to be the focus of one of Jordan's contests.''

''Why not?'' Gar demanded arrogantly. ''I'd win hands down.''

''How do you figure that?'' one of their table-mates demanded.

''I've got the most beautiful girl in the world.''

Beth's face flamed with embarrassment, but she squeezed his hand back anyway. ''Thanks,'' she whispered, for his ears alone.

''I have a lot more to say, if you'll just pay attention.'' His eyes glowed, and Beth allowed herself just a moment to wonder what he'd planned.

The desserts were decadent slices of chocolate-covered cheesecake with a delicately swirled raspberry coulis.

''They did a wonderful job with the meal,'' Nelda Parker murmured to Beth. ''It always tastes better when you don't have to cook it, doesn't it?''

''You've never cooked this before,'' her husband complained.

Nelda sent him a mock frown.

''Folks, if you don't mind, we'll move out of this area and allow our waiters to clear the tables. The Winthrops have kindly opened the library, the solarium and the salon for our use.''

As everyone got up, Gar took the opportunity to

introduce Beth to people she didn't know—his friends, acquaintances and business associates.

"Beth and I are getting married in two weeks," he told them proudly.

"Yes, we saw the invitation." Myles North grinned at Beth and slapped Gar on the shoulder. "I must say, I never thought of your idea for distribution before, though it certainly gets the message across. You can count on Celia and me."

"Thanks, Myles. And don't knock it. If she backs out now, I've got a lot of witnesses to my intentions."

Beth wanted to sink into the floor at the reminder that she'd run out on him once before and left Gar to face a lot of embarrassing questions, but he apparently wasn't aware of her thoughts. After several more introductions, he took her hand and steered her back into the dining area, to a quiet corner where candles still burned among the potted plants she'd arranged earlier.

"I needed a minute alone with my fiancée," he murmured as one hand slid into his jacket pocket. "I have something for you."

Beth suspected a kiss, maybe two. She never even saw the case until he'd snapped it open.

"This is for you. Because I love you very much and I don't want you to forget it. Turn around, okay?"

A dazzlingly bright diamond lay on a bed of pure white satin. When he lifted it out, she saw the silky smooth gold chain. In a daze, Beth obediently turned her back and felt the necklace glide around her neck, felt the touch of his warm fingers at her neck as he fastened it, then turned her around to face him.

"Do you like it?" His voice was husky now, his eyes enquiring as they met hers.

"I love it. It's beautiful. But you've already given me this ring, Gar. I haven't anything for you." She was ashamed that she hadn't even thought of it.

"I don't want anything else. If I have you, that's all I need." He tilted her chin up, flicked the single tear off her cheek and bent his head. "I love you," he whispered. Then he kissed her.

A string quartet started playing in the background, but Beth heard it only vaguely. She was too caught up in this wonderful dream. Her arms lifted around his neck and she laid her head on his shoulder.

"I love you, too, Garrett. Very much."

"And you'll marry me in spite of the invitation thing?" he joked.

"I'll marry you no matter what you do to our wedding." She smiled. Her finger gently traced the laugh lines at the corner of his mouth. "I'm sorry I've been so busy lately. I promise that we'll have plenty of time together soon. In fact, you'll probably get sick of me."

He began to slow dance her around the room. "Never."

They danced for a moment, but it was clear he had something to say. "I have to make something clear, Beth. I want us to be strong together. I don't want anything between us—not money, not people, not anything. I was the one who suggested they hold the ball here tonight."

"You were? Why?" She frowned, but kept dancing, her feet moving automatically to the pretty waltz.

"Because I wanted to erase the memory of that other time. I wanted us to have a new, fresh start here, among our friends and the community." He peered down. "Is it okay?"

"It's wonderful." She sighed happily. "I don't think I've ever enjoyed an evening more."

He whirled her around and into a faster dance as the others began to trickle in and join them on the floor. Several people tried to break in, but Gar refused to let her go.

"Tonight she's all mine," he told them smugly. "Go find your own sweetheart."

"Gar, those are friends of your parents! I don't want to offend them."

"They'll get over it."

It was a wonderfully romantic setting, with the candles glimmering here and there around the perimeter of the room and fresh scent of flowers. Beth couldn't help but relax in the dim lighting with the heavenly music.

It was only Jordan's booming voice that disturbed her. "Ladies and gents, we now have the pleasure of choosing our most romantic couple of the evening. I think we're unanimous in this. Give a round of applause to Miss Beth Ainslow and Mr. Garrett Winthrop."

Beth stared at Gar, her head whirling. *They* were romantic? Ha! If Jordan only knew. But then, maybe he did know. Maybe these people were right. She thrust the doubts and fears aside and went forward with Gar to receive the chocolate cupids.

"May I inform you that Mr. Ty Winthrop, soon to be Chef Winthrop, created our wonderful meal tonight, along with the ice sculptures and the vegetable curly things." He shrugged at his wife. "I couldn't remember the names."

Everyone in the room burst into laughter.

"Ty also made these cupids. Ty, come on out here. We'd like to thank you properly."

Clad in white from head to foot, Ty emerged from the back of the room and bowed, his face wreathed in a smile. His face turned solemn as he accepted Jordan's thanks, shook several hands and then stopped in front of Gar.

"Did you like it?" he asked quietly.

"*You* made all that?" Gar's eyes were huge, his tone disbelieving. "Even the dessert?"

Ty nodded. "Uh-huh. Next year I'm doing something flambéed."

"Next year?" Gar's voice hardened, but Ty didn't seem to notice. The music had started again, and several couples brushed past them in a quick-stepping promenade.

"Yep. They've asked me to do it again. This was great. I can hardly wait to start training."

"Ty, your place is in the bank."

Beth reached out and touched Gar on the arm, willing him not to spoil the night, especially not after his brother's wonderful success. But Ty spoke first.

"No, Gar. The bank is your place. I don't fit in

there. And to tell you the truth, I don't want to. I'm sorry, but I have to be true to myself and my dreams.''

When Ty turned and left the room, Gar followed him, anger marring his handsome face. Beth followed, more worried than she'd ever been. Why was Gar so unwilling to let Ty have his dream? Did he want her to give up the flower shop? Was it unsuitable as a vocation for his wife?

"You can't give up college, training, a future, just to *cook*." Gar's voice was scathing as it rang around the kitchen. "Look at this place. Do you want to be stuck here for the rest of your life, working for someone else, scraping by?"

"Gar, don't." Beth was fully aware of the glowering looks the waiters were throwing his way. "It's his dream, let him live it."

"It's not a dream. It's a nightmare." Garrett stomped from the room.

"I'm sorry, Ty. I'll try to talk to him, get him to see."

"It doesn't matter, Beth. I've made up my mind." Ty turned away to stir a sauce that had just begun to bubble on the stove. "You'll make him happy," he murmured. "You'll be the one he invests his dreams in."

As she left, the words haunted her. *You'll be the one*. She didn't want to be responsible for disappointing Garrett. That was too heavy a burden. Could she give up her dreams for him?

She found him in the solarium, staring out the window. "I'm sorry, Gar."

"Are you?" His eyes chilled her. "You think I should leave him alone, let him pursue this stupidity, let the family down."

"How would he be doing that?" The old bitter feelings resurfaced. Beth tried to squash them down, but they wouldn't be silenced. "What's the matter, Gar? Can't you be proud of a brother who's a chef, even if he becomes the best chef in the world? Is that beneath the dignity of the Winthrop family?"

He refused to be cowed. "It isn't something I'd want to announce to the world, no. He has potential, backing, a heritage. Why throw that all away?"

"Why keep it if it means nothing to you?" she countered, frustration creeping into her voice.

"Don't be so quick to condemn it, Beth. Wouldn't you rather have been raised in a home where there was enough money to put food on the table, pay the bills, and buy you the odd bauble?"

She gasped. "Are you going to be ashamed of me, too, Gar? Does owning a flower shop not rate in your book of acceptable careers? Maybe you'd rather I were more like Cynthia, and wait around for your every beck and call."

"Maybe I would." He raked a hand through his hair as he shook his head. "I'm sorry! Please ignore that. I didn't mean it."

She turned away from him slowly and moved toward the window.

"I think you did mean it, Gar. I think that in spite of your protestations, you really do care about what money can buy." She fingered the necklace. "That's what this is all about, isn't it? Show me off, show off what you can give me. Poor little Beth has come up in the world. I made her what she is to-day.''

She stopped then, swallowing her tears.

''I didn't mean to say that. I love you. I was just angry and disappointed.''

''I know. I disappoint you. I never realized that before—''

The door burst open and Ronnie raced inside, her face flushed. ''Beth, come quick. It's Dad. He's drunk and he's hurt himself.''

Beth ignored Gar's comments. She followed her sister out of the room and across the hall. A thick ring of people stood around the place where Mervyn had fallen to the floor. A shattered wineglass lay at his feet, and Dinah knelt at his side.

''I've done it again,'' he muttered drunkenly, his smile lopsided as he stared into her eyes. ''I was so proud of her, so proud. She's beautiful, my little Bethy. I wanted to show her I knew how to behave. I'm not trash. I can prove it.''

''It's all right, Mervyn. You just slipped. Get up now.'' Dinah urged him to his feet, almost collaps-ing as he leaned on her.

Beth hurried to his side and swung his arm over her shoulder. ''Are you all right, Dad?''

''P-perfectly all right,'' he enunciated clearly. ''I just s-slipped.''

Beth ignored the murmurs that rippled through the crowd. She was shamed, embarrassed and furious. She was lady enough not to show it, but she had to get out of here.

"You're bleeding!" Ronnie pointed to his arm where blood was now soaking the sleeve. "You must have cut yourself."

They walked him slowly out of the room with everyone watching. Beth could have cried. The town drunk and his daughters. What had changed in ten years?

"I feel funny," her father muttered. His face was ashen.

"Sit him here," Dinah ordered. She motioned for one of the waiters. "Get the first-aid kit from the kitchen. And bring a friend. I'm going to need help to take him upstairs."

"How could you do this, Dad? How could you? This was Beth's special night. Gar was trying to make her forget the last time you ruined her party. And now you've done it all over again. Drunk!" Ronnie glared at the man she'd always defended. "I think I hate you for this."

"No, Ronnie, no. Please don't hate me. I just needed a little courage. I only had one drink. Just one. I'm not drunk."

"It's true," Dinah murmured, her face intent as she inspected the cut. "He no doubt feels faint because he's lost a fair bit of blood. And because of the pressure." She straightened, her eyes pinning Beth to her place.

"He wanted to be here for you, to show you he could do this, that he could mix with these people. I knew how uncomfortable he was, how out of place he felt, but I encouraged him anyway because I thought it would help you. I wish I'd never done that.''

"It's not your fault, Mrs. Winthrop." Beth glared at the man she had called Dad. "It's his. He's always spoiling things."

"What did he spoil? Your fairy tale?" Dinah sniffed inelegantly. "Grow up, girl. Life is about reality. Sure, there are lots of snobs in that room, and yes, they were sizing you up. So what?"

"It was bad enough when they knew about the past, but now—" Beth could have groaned at the image most of them had formed.

"Now what? Now they know what you're really like? They know your father has a drinking problem? So what? They know you love my grandson. Or do you?" Her voice dropped to a whisper. "Maybe that's been the problem all along. You love respect and society's view of you more than you do him."

"Gran." Gar's voice was stern.

"She needs to figure it out now. Before it's too late to turn back." Dinah spun back to face Beth and Ronnie. "You girls have a wonderful father. He got buffaloed by some problems, but he's working them through. I suggest you two do the same. Figure out what's important to you."

She motioned the waiters close and directed them to carry Mervyn up the stairs.

"Garrett, go explain that Mr. Ainslow has cut himself and requires a doctor. Tell them to go on with the party. We'll be down later."

Gar glanced helplessly from her to Beth, but finally he went. Alone, Beth glanced at Ronnie.

"Did Ty give you the van key?" When her sister nodded, she moved toward the entry as though her insides were frozen. "Good. Let's go."

"You can't go now! The best part is still coming." Ronnie's eyes begged her to reconsider.

But Beth had her coat on and was already at the front door.

"No, I think the best part's over," she whispered. "And it's time for Cinderella to get to work. The dream has turned into a nightmare. And it's time to end it. I don't belong here," she murmured sadly, glancing once more around the beautiful room. "I never did. Why did it take so long for me to see that?"

"Beth, Gar loves you!"

"Does he?" Beth shook her head. "I think he loves somebody I can never be—his idea of a fairy princess. Well, I'm no princess. I know that now."

# *Chapter Twelve*

Beth peered through the swirling snow that almost obliterated the view. Some Valentine's Day this was turning out to be.

"A half a mile, they said." She pressed her foot down infinitesimally, and held her breath as the van veered slightly sideways. She righted it and continued down the finger-drifted road. "It's got to be here somewhere."

Up ahead, out of the early evening darkness, a shadow loomed, the dull glow of yellow lights signaling the farmhouse.

It took only a few minutes to carry the big white box of crimson red roses to the door, but substantially longer to listen to Bill Harrison's kind words.

"You'll never know how much this means," he murmured, checking to be sure no one was behind him. "Belinda's been so sick after the chemo that I didn't dare take the time to run in to town. Your delivery is a real blessing." He pulled open the box slowly, his eyes growing bigger by the moment.

Beth felt a supreme sense of satisfaction. *This is why I want to be a florist,* she told Gar silently. She'd taken the time to choose the best blooms she carried. They lay nestled in the layers of rich green fern, a big white bow holding them all together.

"You didn't have to go to all this trouble," he whispered, his eyes glossy.

"I wanted to. Tell Belinda Happy Valentine's from Ronnie and me, too, will you? And tell her that I hope she feels better soon."

"I will." He pumped her hand heartily. "I can see why Gar wants to marry you," he murmured. "You're a perfect addition to Oakburn. You really are concerned about the people who live here. We need folks like you to provide these caring services."

"Thanks, Bill," she murmured. "Thanks a lot. 'Bye now." And she backed down the stairs, her heart singing through its sadness.

"Do you think maybe you should stay here for a while? Just 'til the storm eases? Visibility is getting pretty bad." Bill's lined forehead pleated in worry.

Beth shook her head determinedly. "I'll keep pushing on."

Bill had enough to worry about. She wasn't going to add to it. Besides, he needed this special time with his wife.

"I've got one more delivery to make, Bill. Then

I'll hightail it home. Thanks, anyway." She waved and then scrambled back across the drifts to her van.

"Okay, then. But take it easy." Bill waved before closing the door.

*"There's no other way to take it. Why tonight, God? Couldn't you have waited an hour or so before you threw this blizzard at us?"* She muttered the words as she steered left, then right, and finally made it back to the highway. It was dangerous to stop, but she'd be okay on this side road for a minute while she checked directions.

"Three and a half miles south, left for another seven. Gotcha." She tucked the note into the visor, checked carefully, then proceeded onto the highway.

"Wonder why it has to be eleven roses?" she asked herself, musing on the odd order. "Usually they ask for an even dozen. Hey, I know. It's probably for the Parkers, they've got about that many kids!"

She amused herself by talking out loud, speculating on the owner of the oddly scrawled initials.

"I'm going to have to teach Ronnie how to print these things. Yeow!" She eased around the huge drift of snow and inched forward, intent on finding the next turnoff.

"It was nice of Bill to say such kind things, nice to be appreciated." She wondered absently if anyone could ever fully appreciate how much satisfaction she derived from her work. "This has been a very successful month. I guess the good citizens of

Oakburn haven't heard the latest scandal about me. Or maybe they don't care.''

Now there was a thought. She considered it more closely. Did she think about Isobel's awful history every time she went in Fenstein's to buy groceries? Of course not! She liked going there because the people were friendly and the quality was good. That was how Isobel and Marty stayed in business—they met a need.

It was the same with her, Beth decided as she clamped her lips tight and shoved her van through the mounting drifts. Her customers came into Enchanted Florist because of what she'd made of it and herself, because she gave them a fair return for their money. Sometimes she even went a little beyond fair, she mused, thinking about Belinda's hidden chocolate surprise.

She tried to puzzle it out more thoroughly, as her vehicle slipped and slid around the corner. Now she was heading east and on the last seven miles of her delivery trek.

''So in effect, they like doing business with me because of *me,* not because of what Dad did, or Gar does, or even for Ronnie's sake.'' She'd never thought of it that way before.

A clear patch of highway opened up as the snow blew across it. Beth accelerated, taking advantage of the clear pavement.

And because of what God had done for her.

Her worth had nothing to do with her roots, or even what she'd done. Her worth was in her value as His child. No matter how hard she worked, she couldn't improve on that.

She straightened suddenly. All her long hours, her need to prove herself, her drive to succeed—all of that was wasted?

"Yes," she whispered, staring at the white vastness before her. "Because I am who I am due to God's grace. I never thought of that before!"

It was wonderful, exhilarating, freeing. She wasn't worthless no matter what happened, because God had given her a royal heritage.

"It's not something I've done, it's something He's done."

Her eyes widened as the knowledge seeped in. She was worthy of Gar's love, of her father's love, of God's love, because He said so. It was that easy. She could stop trying to prove herself because, in reality, all the workaholism in the world didn't matter.

She recalled what had happened earlier this afternoon. "Beth, I didn't mean I hated you working. I like the fact that you've learned to be independent, to run your own business. I'm proud of you." Gar's words had clearly penetrated the thick back door of her store. But he didn't have to yell. She was standing right inside, tears rolling down her cheeks.

"But to tell you the truth, it wouldn't matter if you were penniless and as dumb as a stump. I don't care about any of the other stuff, Beth. I care about you, what's inside you, what makes you who you are. None of that has anything to do with your dad or my brother. I love you because you're Beth. I'm just jealous of the time everything else takes away from us."

Jealous? He was jealous? Beth had scoffed at the idea.

"Go away, Garrett. I have a lot of work to do. That's what I do—work. I'm not a society deb. I have responsibilities, duties. I can't just ignore them to play with you."

The memory of her scathing remarks make her flush with embarrassment. He'd insisted she open the door.

"What is it? Can't you see I'm busy?"

His face was white, pinched, worried. "I know. And you don't want to do this in front of Ronnie. I understand."

"Don't mind me. I'm going into the cooler. Let me know when you're done." Grinning from ear to ear, Ronnie had yanked the big door shut.

"Beth, will you just listen to me for a minute?"

"I don't think there's much more to say." She'd ruined a floral arrangement because her hands were shaking too much. "I think I've heard everything I want to hear."

"I think you heard only what you wanted to hear," he retorted, spots of red on his cheeks.

Implying what? That she was too *dumb* to understand?

"Oh, I got it," she assured him, fury shooting the words from her mouth. "I got it all."

Gar's face was drawn, his eyes sad. "This isn't

what I wanted," he told her quietly. "I wanted a special night, a time you would remember. I wanted you to feel on top of the world, not because you were marrying me, but because that's how God's child should feel."

She couldn't say anything.

"This thing you have about proving yourself, it isn't necessary to the rest of us. I love you. I don't know how else to tell you that. I don't care what your father did or what my father did. I don't care what people say, I love you. And the only thing I want is for us to be together." He reached up to touch her, his fingers gentle. "I love you, Beth Ainslow."

"We can't be together when there's this gap between us, Garrett. I will always be the girl from the wrong side of the tracks. I'm not your fairy princess."

His face fell, his hand dropped away from her cheek. "To me you are," he whispered. "And the only thing that's between us is what you put there. It's a barrier that only you can remove. Please think about the future. Our future."

"There is no future for us, Garrett. It's over."

"I'm not giving up, Beth. I haven't waited this long for you just to walk away. I'll be waiting, no matter how long it takes you to see the truth."

Now, as she drove along, the truth finally dawned. Even after the scene at Fairwinds, Gar wanted to marry her. To him it truly didn't matter whether her father was a fall-down drunk or a man who'd simply slipped on a bit of paper. That wasn't part of the equation. All Garrett Winthrop cared about was Beth Ainslow.

Whether she succeeded or fell flat on her face, Gar would still love her. Whether she made mistakes or didn't, whether her father started drinking again or not—none of it mattered.

Love had nothing to do with what happened outside of her, it had to do with what went on in her heart. Gar had loved her for over ten years, and he'd promised to keep on loving her. So would her dad. So would God.

"Why didn't I see this before?" she asked herself in frustration. "Why do I always come back to what people think of me—?"

It was a moment before Beth felt the telltale slide of the rear wheels and knew she was in trouble. Though she fought to stay on the road, the huge snowdrift at the side sucked her off the pavement and into its arms with a welcoming *whoosh*.

Carefully she rocked the vehicle back and forth, whispering a word of prayer as the tires spun uselessly on the soft, wet snow. She kept at it, even though she knew it was futile. The reality of her situation was too dangerous to think about. But when the van refused to budge, she was forced to acknowledge the truth.

She was stuck out here in the countryside, with no help for miles.

"Great." She checked the gas gauge and frowned. She had enough to let it run for a little while, but she couldn't afford to let the tank get dangerously low. Who knew how long she'd have to wait for assistance? And would it come in time?

As the van purred, Beth suddenly realized just how dark it had become. Her headlights were buried in the snowbank. No matter how hard she peered through the windshield, she could see nothing.

If by chance someone did come looking, how would they find her?

She undid her seat belt, then eased the door slightly open. The bitter cold wind whistled in, making short work of the heat she'd built up inside. Beth forced herself out of her seat and into the snow, hoping to spot a familiar landmark, another vehicle, something.

There was only darkness, howling wind and snow that whipped and stung her bare face.

"I'm caught out here in the middle of a blizzard," she whispered to herself. "And nobody knows it."

She slipped back inside the van, allowing the blast of heat from the ducts to warm her icy fingers. When she was almost warm, she switched off the engine. The gas gauge was going down awfully fast.

*I'm in trouble here, God. Big trouble. I stormed out without giving a thought to something like this. I was so sure I had to get away.* She twisted around in her seat, and, with the help of the overhead light, considered the area at the back.

Only one box remained. One box with eleven pale yellow roses carefully laid inside. She lifted a floormat and arranged it over the box, hoping to protect the fragile blooms as much as possible from the cold that was seeping in.

"Ronnie will notice that I haven't come back. She'll get someone. They'll come looking. Whoever is expecting this delivery will be furious." She tried to cheer herself with the thoughts.

But deep inside she knew it was hopeless. She'd demanded that everyone leave her alone. And they had.

"Why didn't I let Ronnie put that cell phone in here?" she asked herself grimly. "At least I could have phoned for help."

But there was no point dealing in "ifs" and "ands" now. It was too late. She'd raced off, left her friends staring and wondering, dumped Gar and hightailed it out of there so fast, they were probably glad to be rid of her.

It was a pattern. She'd done it often. Run away, ignored things, pretended she could fix them herself. But she couldn't fix this. This time she'd really blown it.

"What if I die out here?" The thought made her cringe.

"I never told Gar that it almost tore me apart to leave here back then. I never told him that the dream in my heart never quite died, even when we were so far apart."

She thought of Ronnie, working so hard to ensure Beth was proud of her, spending hours in the shop when she should have been out with the other kids, having fun. Beth had wanted so much for Ronnie—

all the things she hadn't had herself. Most of all, she'd wanted her sister to grow up carefree.

Instead she'd burdened Ronnie with guilt and obligations. The knowledge ate at her, and she glanced heavenward, her heart heavy.

"Okay, I blew it. All of it." She shifted, turned on the ignition and shivered until warm air finally poured in. "I'm lousy at running things, including my own life. I thought I could fix things, begin again, earn respect and a place in Oakburn. I thought I could prove that I'm good enough. And I can't."

She admitted the truth with a clogged-up throat. Her father's actions last night had proven that she had no control over what he or anyone else did or said. She couldn't make him into the kind of father she believed would be respectable any more than she could make Ronnie into an airhead who would abandon Beth to go have a good time.

It was the same with Gar. "I did want the fairy tale," she muttered, staring out through the snow-spattered windshield. "I wanted him to be someone he's not, to sweep me off my feet like some kind of prince. But I wouldn't let myself believe that I was worth it. I had to prove to him that I was more than adequate as a candidate for his wife."

She considered that. But why? *Why do I keep getting myself into these situations? What don't I understand what You're trying to teach me, God?*

The engine sputtered and died, cutting off all sound except the howl of the wind outside the van. Beth shivered, hugging her coat a little closer.

Who was in control now?

The words penetrated her brain with the clarity of a ringing bell. Beth frowned, trying to understand why she'd thought of that.

"God is in control," she whispered, reciting the only words she could remember from a song her sister often sang. "'Who makes the sun rise and set, the ocean tides wax and wane, the wind whistle or die down?'" The questions poured into her brain, demanding a response she could not withhold.

"God does." Beth acknowledged it out loud. "But I've never denied that."

Haven't you? Haven't you been trying to control everyone and everything, to make them fit your will? Haven't you just refused the gift of love God sent because it didn't fit your narrow perceptions?

Beth had never before thought of Gar's love as a gift from God, and the idea intrigued her.

Garrett Winthrop didn't put on airs, didn't pretend to be someone he wasn't, didn't even ask her to be someone other than who she was. Instead, Gar had insisted that he loved her in spite of everything she'd done. He didn't seem to care if he was in her shabby apartment at Wintergreen or dancing at Fairwinds. His love remained steady, burning brightly, enclosing her in its warmth. Wasn't that a love worth saving?

Gar didn't care if she was the belle of the ball, if she wore jeans or designer dresses, or that her father had taken a drink when he shouldn't have. He was more concerned with the important things. The person inside was what mattered to him.

That's why he'd been able to accept Mervyn when Beth hadn't. That was why he'd been able to acknowledge Denis as a part of her past life and move on. He cared about her, her happiness, her contentment.

"All I've cared about is the outward stuff, the appearances, the look of things." The knowledge was sobering. "I worked so hard to be acceptable, worthy, on the same level. And it doesn't matter!"

She exulted in the sudden knowledge.

"None of it matters! God loves me in spite of who and what I am. Because he loves me, Gar thinks I'm worthy. Dad loves me because I'm his daughter, not because of what I have or haven't done. I can't do anything to improve on that."

A weight lifted off her shoulders, and Beth sagged under the freedom of it.

"I can't earn their love," she mumbled, flexing her fingers as the cold crept through her gloves. "There's nothing I can do to make them care for me any more than they already do. And all that I'm doing is pushing them away."

She bowed her head as tears came to her eyes. She remembered Gar's call to the store while she and Ronnie had been loading the last of the bouquets into the van.

"Tell him we're finished," she'd ordered Ronnie, her cheeks red with embarrassment. "Tell him to find someone who won't ruin his life, someone with less baggage. As soon as I can sell this place, we're leaving.''

Ronnie pleaded for her to just listen, to give the man a chance. But Beth hadn't done that, hadn't wanted to hear it. Instead she'd filled the last order and taken off.

"Why?" she asked God. "Why do I always push love away?"

The answer stole into her heart. *You won't trust. You won't let go of the controls.*

As snow piled up on the windshield and the wind snuck in through the cracks, Beth wept for the foolishness of her life. Here she was, lost in a blizzard, because she had to run the show. It was a fitting end.

"I'm sorry, God. I always said that I believed You had good things in store for me, but I never walked the walk. All this time you've been trying to get my attention, and I've been too busy running the show." She gulped down a sob, determined to say what was in her heart.

"Okay, God. From here on in, You run the show. Whatever You have in store for me, I'll accept with a grateful heart.

"I love Gar. And though he may hate me now, I'm asking You for one more chance to tell him. He'll probably never forgive me for running out on him at the party, for shutting him out at the store, for not answering his call, but that doesn't matter. I still owe him the truth. Please, just give me one more chance.''

It was cold, so cold. Beth shivered and tried to stop her teeth from chattering. How long had she been here? An hour? Two or three? She didn't know. All she knew was that she couldn't withstand the cold for much longer. Already her feet and hands were going numb in their thin coverings.

"Please help me," she murmured again. Her eyelids dropped. She was tired. So tired. Maybe if she slept just a little while.

She'd just begun the most wonderful dream when someone wrenched open her door. Freezing cold winter wind whipped across her cheeks, and Beth huddled into the seat, forming her body into a tight ball.

"S'cold," she muttered through clenched teeth. "Close the door."

"I'm going to," a dear, gruff voice muttered. Big strong arms slid under her knees and around her back. "As soon as I get you out of here. C'mon, Beth, it's time to go. This time you're not running any farther."

She felt herself being carried, heard a wheezing grunt, and snuggled closer to the warmth. "I like this dream," she giggled, rubbing her cheek against the soft wool fabric. "You even sound like him."

"Like who?" The voice was only half amused.

"Like Gar." She sighed. "He's my Prince Charming. Isn't that silly? And I'm the princess. Only I never told him how much I loved him. Wasn't that a stupid mistake? I got sidetracked and forgot the most important part. Without Gar, nothing else matters." A tear rose to her lashes, but Beth couldn't be bothered to lift a hand to remove it. Instead, she let the sadness of the dream overwhelm her.

"He was my fiancé. For a little while, anyway."

"He still is. That part isn't changing until we get married, Beth. I told you, I don't give up easily."

Beth forced her eyelids open, staring as she focused on his beloved face. She gasped, then lifted one hand to touch his cheek.

"It's not a dream—it is you!"

"It's me, all right. You didn't think I was going to leave my future wife buried in a snowbank, did you?" He tugged open the door of a vehicle Beth didn't recognize, and set her carefully on the seat. "I like a white wedding as much as the next groom, but this is going a little far." He laughed at her confused frown.

For several moments Beth couldn't move, couldn't say anything as he tucked her in. There was so much she needed to tell him, to explain. But it would wait. Only one thing was important.

"I love you, Garrett Algernon Winthrop."

He grinned, a big hearty grin that did nothing to conceal the smugness in his eyes. "I know. I've been counting on that to get us through this whole mix-up. Sit tight, I'll be right back." With that, he slammed her door shut.

Beth sat there and let the heat from the vents blow over her. Little by little the warmth seeped into her cold body and the dream-like trance melted away.

But the storm was still raging around them, and she waited anxiously for Gar to return.

She heard him open the back door, and then he was easing into the seat beside her, his face red and wind-chafed.

"Are you okay? You didn't hurt anything when you slid off the road?" His eyes anxiously searched her face, her body, looking for damage.

"I'm fine. But how did you know…" She let the words die away as he leaned over and kissed her hard on the lips.

"Just relax. We'll talk as soon as we get home."

Home? Where was home? The heat was making her drowsy and she couldn't concentrate. Instead, she closed her eyes and let it all go.

Hadn't she given it all to God? He was in charge now.

# *Chapter Thirteen*

Gar pressed his foot on the accelerator and steered the Jeep straight through the building snowdrifts as they climbed the steep pass. His heart filled with praise as he got closer and closer to home.

*Thank you, God. Thank you for second chances. And thirds. I promise, I won't blow it this time.* He drove up to the door, as close as he could get, and left the engine running.

In a matter of minutes he had Beth inside and huddled in front of a fire. "Stay put. I'll be back in a minute."

As quickly as he could, he put the Jeep in the garage, picked up the flowers and walked back inside.

Beth was where he'd left her, her eyes closed. Satisfied that she was breathing normally, he poured out two mugs of the hot chocolate he'd made earlier and set them on the coffee table. Then he retrieved the flowers.

"Beth?"

She opened her eyes and blinked at him, glancing around to get her bearings. "Here? How did I get here?"

"I brought you here. You were on your way, anyway." He held out the roses. "You were delivering your own bouquet."

She stared at the flowers. "You ordered those?"

He nodded. "I'm the last stop on your Valentine run. I hope you like them. They're from the best florist in town."

"I'm also the only florist in town," she quipped, a faint smile twitching at her bluish lips. "Why eleven?"

"It's eleven years since I proposed." His eyes twinkled. "And yellow because I'm making a solid gold promise. I'm promising you joy and love. No matter what."

Gar reached out and helped her remove her coat, boots and gloves. Then he knelt in front of her.

"I love you, Beth Ainslow. When I couldn't find you tonight, I almost went crazy. Why did you run away from me? Why did you say it was over between us? What did I do wrong?"

She smiled and reached out, her soft fingers tracing his jaw. "Nothing," she whispered, tears forming at the corners of her expressive eyes. "You did nothing wrong. It's me. I've been working so hard to make myself worthy of being your wife that I forgot the most important thing." She leaned forward, cupping his face in both hands.

"I love you, Garrett. I love you more than I ever thought possible. I'm not running away again. I think I've done enough of that."

"I'm sorry your dad let you down, Beth. And I'm sorry I didn't understand about Ty. But I'm not going to let their problems come between us. Ty's old enough to find his own way. I know I can't live his life for him. I haven't done such a hot job of managing my own."

She pressed her forefinger against his lips. "Those things don't matter. I can't control my father's drinking any more than you can control Ty's future. They both have to do that themselves."

He frowned. "But isn't that what made you run away? I thought, well—" He hesitated, hating to say the words.

"You thought I was embarrassed by the scene Dad made. That's what you thought, isn't it?" She waited a moment for his nod. "In a way you were right. I was embarrassed. And I thought that his behavior, along with a whole lot of other things, disqualified me from becoming your wife."

"Beth," he gasped, "I don't care about that!"

She smiled. "I know that now. God showed me how wrong I'd been tonight when I was stuck in the van. I've been trying to mold everybody into the place I thought they should be. I guess I've been doing it for a long time."

"Why?" Gar wasn't sure he understood any of this.

"I wanted life to be the way I'd planned. When it didn't turn out that way, I tried to manipulate things and people to make it go my way. I had this idea, you see—" she shook her head in disgust "—I wanted my dad, Ronnie, Ty, even you, to be somebody that you're not. I got so consumed with the appearance of things, I missed…love."

He tipped back on his haunches and considered what she was saying. The fire crackled and blazed behind him, but he focused on the small delicate woman who sat curled up in front of him.

"Did you mean what you said?" he managed at last, aware that he was holding his breath as he waited for her response.

"About loving you?" She smiled, her face seemingly lighting up from within. "I've never meant anything more. I do love you, Gar. And if I embarrass you with my lower-class manners or lack of social graces, then I'm really sorry, but you'll just have to accept it. This is who I am. Beth Ainslow, born on the wrong side of the tracks."

"Embarrass me?" He felt a faint stirring of anger. "When I'm with you I feel like the proudest man in the world. What does any of that stuff matter?" Something twigged, and Gar took a deep breath. "The only thing that would really embarrass me is if you didn't show up at the altar next Saturday."

"Next Saturday?" She laughed and shook her head. "No, you mean the week after, and it's a Sunday."

Gar shifted uncomfortably, wishing he could avoid her eyes. "Actually, I *do* mean next Saturday.'' He swallowed. "You remember those invitations I had dropped from that plane?'' She nodded, so he continued. "Well—that is, the, er, the printer made an error that I didn't catch. It seems everyone has been invited to our wedding next Saturday at eleven o'clock in the morning.''

Gar sat there staring at the carpet, waiting for her to blast him for his carelessness. When she didn't say anything, he finally glanced up. His eyes widened at her shaking shoulders, and he got to his feet, tugging her into his arms to comfort her. How could he have been so stupid?

"Oh, Beth, honey. I'm sorry! I didn't mean to spoil everything. The embarrassment doesn't matter, sweetheart. We can get married whenever you want. The only thing that matters is that you love me as much as I love you.'' He stopped, took a second look and then frowned. "Beth?''

He lifted her chin and found her eyes glinting with laughter. She burst into loud boisterous chuckles. Gar sagged in relief. At least she wasn't bawling. But he still couldn't figure out what was so all-fired funny.

"I don't think it's that big a joke,'' he muttered when she wouldn't stop chortling.

"It's hilarious,'' she said, wiping tears of mirth from her eyes. "If you knew what I'd just told God, out there in that blizzard, you'd see.''

"What did you tell Him?'' He waited, arms looped around her waist while she regained control. "Well?''

"I told Him that I was taking my hands off the

controls, that He was in charge and I'd follow wherever He led." She hiccuped a laugh. "It seems that He's leading up to the altar next Saturday."

Gar shook his head, confused by this woman and her calm acceptance of their future. "I love you, Beth, more than life itself. But sometimes you make me a little crazy. Are you saying you'll marry me next week, without all the pomp and circumstance I had planned for the week after?"

Beth sobered at that. Her eyes roved over his face, and he watched as the love lit those blue depths.

"Of course I'm going to marry you, Garrett. You're my Prince Charming. You rescued me from the snow and carried me to safety. I'm not crazy, you know! I'm not letting a man like you go."

She stopped teasing then, her eyes steady. "Nothing on this earth will prevent me from walking up that aisle next week, Garrett Winthrop. I love you and, pomp and circumstance notwithstanding, I intend to marry you at the very first opportunity. Which just happens to be next Saturday."

"Oh." He digested that for a minute and then prepared to push his luck. "And can we live here, in this house that I built for you?" He didn't wait for her response, but rushed on. "I've planned and dreamed and schemed for us to live here for so long. I've pictured you sitting in front of the fire with me, climbing the hills on a summer evening, having a picnic with our kids out by the river."

She was crying again. Gar sighed. Would he ever get the hang of this?

"It doesn't matter, Beth. Not really. We can live

anywhere. As long as I have you, I don't care about any of it.''

''Well, I do! I want it all. Of course we're going to live here.'' She fingered her ring, the garnet he'd given her, which sparkled on her finger. ''I want to share the future with you for as long as we have together. And we'll live here, even if we have to shuffle things around a bit. Love is worth some compromise, don't you think?''

Gar bent his head and kissed her, a soul-stirring, heartfelt kiss that told her how much he loved her. Then he showed her all through the house, explaining every carefully thought-out detail.

Eventually they wandered back to the fire and sat down on the big hearth rug, side by side, sipping the now cooled chocolate.

''My grandmother was right,'' he murmured into the silence a long time later. ''She said you and she were two of a kind and she was right.''

''I love your grandmother, and I take that as a compliment, but I'm not sure how you arrived there.'' Beth shifted against his side, her hand slipping around his waist. ''Explain, please.''

''Dinah was the eldest of ten children. Her father was a coal miner and they were dirt poor. She always minimizes their poverty, but believe me, they were impoverished. Her mother died when Dinah was twelve.''

''Okay, that's a coincidence.'' Beth frowned, her eyes on the flickering bed of coals. ''What else?''

''Dinah took on the role of mother and raised every one of those kids until all of her brothers and sisters had left home. Then she took care of her father and made a little extra money by taking in laundry and sewing until he, too, passed on. Then, when her duty was finally complete, with no place to go and not a dime in her pocket, she looked for work.'' He smiled, pressing a kiss to her hair. "Dinah was a survivor, just like you.''

"What else?''

"Well, she met Randolph Winthrop when she worked as a maid in his house. He fell in love with her and married her six months later, against his parents' wishes.''

"Another similarity.'' Beth seemed lost in thought.

"They were blissfully happy. I used to watch them, snuggled together under the mistletoe at Christmas, or giggling over a box of chocolates he'd given her for Valentine's Day, and I'd think, That's how I want my marriage to be.''

"They only had one child?''

"My father, yes.'' Gar nodded. "But they adored him. And when my father had me, they were like kids. I had some wonderful times at their house, playing hide-and-seek with Dinah in the old wardrobes and helping her in her rose garden. She never cared when I stopped over or what I wanted to talk about. She always put down whatever she was doing and listened to me. People were always coming to her for advice, and I used to wish they wouldn't so I'd have more time to have her to myself.''

"You loved her.''

"Yes. I still do. She's given me so much happiness. When I used to sit in church on those hard benches, I'd look around for something to do, and Dinah would always wink at me. It was our secret wink. I'd lean down to tie my shoe, and she'd pass me a mint. She always had a mint for me, for any kid that asked.''

Beth sat there, thinking about the woman who'd come from nothing and eventually inherited millions of dollars. But better than all of that, she had the priceless gift of love.

''I asked her once if she wasn't sad that she hadn't met Grandpa earlier, that they hadn't had more children. She said God had given her exactly what she needed to help her grow.''

''Did a lot of her friends know about her past?'' Beth couldn't help asking. The tiny delicate woman she'd met seemed so unlike a woman who'd grown up in poverty and need.

''I'm sure everybody knew. She never hid it. She said that growing up in need gave you a better perspective on what was really important. To Dinah, love was always more important, and she never lets you forget that we are all God's children.'' He glanced down at her. ''Am I boring you?''

''No, of course not. I was just thinking how wonderful it is to have all these memories of her. She's hosted world leaders, been visited by people in high places, and yet you think of her as a warm, caring woman who took the time to play with you.'' She grimaced. ''It's a lesson for me to look beyond what I have to what I'm giving, what memories there will be of me. It sure took a long time to learn.''

She glanced down at her unusual ring and played with it, then smiled when Gar tilted her head to look into her eyes.

"But I'm learning fast. And I think I've finally got my priorities straight. No matter what happens to us, Gar, I'm not going to forget that when it comes to loving you, nothing else is more important. I'd love to live here with you, darling. It already feels like home. This is where I want to begin our legacy of love. We can keep my place at Wintergreen for emergencies. Like tonight."

He kissed her again, his touch telling her how much her words meant to him.

When they finally broke apart, they were content to sit staring into the fire, dreaming dreams of a future filled with happiness.

"Garrett?"

"Mm-hmm." He lifted his head to look at her. "What is it?"

"What *exactly* did you have planned for our wedding?"

Gar burst out laughing, his eyes glittering. "You said you'd leave it up to me," he reminded.

Beth swallowed her frustration. *Let go of the controls,* she reminded herself.

"I am leaving it up to you. Really. I just wanted a hint. You know, an idea of what to expect."

She sighed when he shook his head.

"Oh, Beth! When will you learn to trust me?"

"I do trust you," she insisted. "I'm just wondering what kind of dress I need to get."

Gar snorted. "The dress doesn't matter. It's the

bride and groom that are important. The prince and princess are what make the fairy tale."

Beth relaxed against his arm, her heart winging skyward. "You're right," she whispered, praying a prayer for heavenly help that would see her through the next busy days. "I love you."

"The feeling, my darling Miss Ainslow, is entirely mutual."

# Chapter Fourteen

"**Y**ou've got to admit that it's different." Mary-ann nudged Caitlin in the ribs, nodding at the big heart-shaped pew markers. "He's really taken this Valentine's theme to heart, so to speak."

Caitlin giggled, juggling her daughter on her knee. "I love the canopy," she whispered back. "It's so romantic. Is it time for us to go get her yet?"

"She said she wanted a minute with her dad. I'd say that's about up." Caitlin rose, handed her daughter to the baby-sitter, and smoothed down her red-satin dress. "I have no clue where he found these on such short notice, but they're actually quite lovely."

Maryann nodded, resplendent in a matching gown. "Did you get a look at Beth's gown?"

"Uh-uh. It hadn't arrived last night when I stopped in. She was strangely calm about it all, though. Said the dress wasn't important." Caitlin handed Maryann her bouquet. "She's certainly got the right attitude."

"Let's go get her. It's time."

When they opened the door, Beth was standing by a window, studying the view. She turned and smiled, her face serene, radiant under the thin white veiling.

"It's snowing again," she murmured.

"Don't remind us! How lucky you are to be escaping it all." Maryann straightened her skirt and sighed. "You look so beautiful, Beth. This dress is perfect."

"It is rather nice, isn't it? Dinah found it. Would you believe a friend of hers is a designer?" She twirled around, sending the gossamer skirt billowing around her ankles. "And this little hat just fits. I've never worn a hat before." She sighed with sheer pleasure.

"Beth, are you ready?" Ronnie bustled into the room, her tall slim figure clothed in red velvet, just like the others. "Gar is waiting."

"Then let's not keep him standing there!" Beth picked up her sheaf of red and creamy white roses and smiled. "I'm ready."

"You look totally awesome," Ronnie breathed, her eyes teary. "I love you, sis."

"I love you, too, Ron. But if you give the Winthrops any trouble, my name will be mud." Beth grinned. "Not that I'm worrying. Dinah assured me that she and Dad will be in complete control."

"Go!" Ronnie ordered with a mock grimace. "You and Gar deserve each other."

Beth waited until Caitlin, then Maryann, then Ronnie had preceded her. Then she smiled at her father, wrapped her arm in his and whispered, "Let's go, Dad."

He hesitated a moment, his eyes soft. "I love you, honey."

"I know. I love you, too."

"I always did." He looked saddened.

Beth couldn't bear to see it on her wedding day. She squeezed his arm and grinned. "I always knew that, too. Come on, Dad. I'm ten, no eleven, years late doing this. I want to be Mrs. Garrett Winthrop before another hour passes."

He squeezed her hand, then carefully led her down the aisle. When they reached Gar, Mervyn placed his daughter's hand in Garrett's welcoming one. "Take care of her," he whispered.

"I will," Gar promised, smiling from ear to ear.

The pastor opened his book to begin the ceremony, but a resounding boom forestalled his delivery.

Beth glanced at Gar and sighed, noting the red flush on his cheekbones as he frowned at Ty. "What was that?" she asked in a hushed whisper.

"A canon. It was supposed to go off *after* our vows. Sorry, darling."

"That's all ri—"

A loud squawking of birds rang through the sanctuary. Beth raised one eyebrow at Gar.

"Doves," he whispered back. "I'm sorry, Beth.

I meant to make this wedding the talk of the town, but nothing's going right. People are going to be talking about us all right.''

Beth glanced upward, a small private smile curving the corners of her mouth. *Funny,* she thought. *Very funny, Lord.*

Then she turned to Gar, her smile fixed firmly in place. It really didn't matter, she decided. Nothing could spoil the wonder and beauty of their love.

She squeezed his hand and turned to the minister. ''We're ready now.''

The rest of the wedding went off without a hitch. But the wedding reception had to be postponed because of the impending snowstorm. Which in turn meant that the bride and groom couldn't get away to the Caribbean.

Undaunted, Beth changed from her finery into an old pair of jeans and a warm sweater, while Gar unloaded the supply-filled car. She wandered through the house he'd built for her, amazed at the detail he'd put into each room. When he returned, she was waiting beside the fire.

''I'm sorry we couldn't fly out,'' he murmured, wrapping his arms around her waist. ''I really wanted to spend two weeks alone with you on a tropical island.''

Beth shrugged, leaning against him. ''We can't control the weather, Gar. We have to take what God gives us and work with it. Besides, I'm marooned with you here, on this snowy hill, miles away from civilization. What more could I ask for?''

She was about to kiss him when the lights flickered, then went out.

"I never said a word," Gar chuckled, holding her close as the faint glow from the fire lit up the room.

Beth pulled a blanket from the sofa and spread it before the fire. When Gar was seated, she handed him a mug of steaming hot chocolate and tinkled hers against it.

"You know, when I gave up control in the snowstorm and promised God that I'd rely on Him, I never realized exactly what that meant. Two snowstorms in February, a misfired cannon, birds that won't fly away, and power that doesn't work." She shook her head. "Are you expecting anything else?"

Gar reached over and took away her mug, setting it carefully on a nearby table. He wrapped both arms around her, bent his head down and touched her mouth with his.

"It doesn't really matter, does it?" he whispered.

Beth kissed him back, a thrill of delight coursing through her. "Not a bit," she assured him softly. "Not one single bit. I love you, Mr. Winthrop."

"And I love you, Mrs. Winthrop. I've been waiting for you for ten, make that eleven, long years."

\* \* \* \* \*

Dear Reader,

Welcome back to my fantasy town of Oakburn. I hope you've enjoyed my three brides and the wonderful blessings they've found, though they had to wait ten long years! Beth's courage in returning to Oakburn and facing all the problems that lay in wait for her are a reminder to me, too. I see in Beth's growth a pattern we could all follow. If we will just believe that God, our loving heavenly Father, wants more for us than we can imagine, it would be so easy to be patient and wait on His guidance. But Beth's story proves that in spite of trying to find her own solutions, God worked through her circumstances and gave her the most wondrous gift of love.

As we approach the month of valentines and Cupids, I wish you much chocolate, many flowers, but better than all of that, a heart full to overflowing with the love of a God who is enough.

I'd love to hear from you. Please write me at: Box 639, Nipawin, Saskatchewan, Canada S0E 1E0.